Graded Readers

The Prisoner of Zenda

Anthony Hope

Level 4
2750 plus headwords

Retold by
Bani Roy Choudhury

STERLING PUBLISHERS (P) LTD.
A-59, Okhla Industrial Area, Phase-II, New Delhi-110020
Phone : 26387070, 26386209; Fax : 91-11-26383788
e-mail: mail@sterlingpublishers.com
www.sterlingpublishers.com

© 2005, Sterling Publishers Private Limited
Reprint 2010

All rights are reserved. No part of this publication may be reproduced, stored in a retrieval system or transmitted, in any form or by any means, mechanical, photocopying, recording or otherwise, without prior written permission of the publisher.

Printed at Sterling Publishers Pvt. Ltd., New Delhi-110020.

Introduction

Sir Anthony Hope (1863-1933) was an English novelist. Born in London and named Anthony Hope Hopkins, he was educated at Marlborough and won a scholarship to Oxford.

He became a barrister in 1887 and began his writing career at around the same time. He began by contributing articles to various periodicals. He gave up his practice at the Bar in 1894 in order to write full-time, and in April of the same year, he produced *The Prisoner of Zenda,* a thrilling and romantic story set in an imaginary country, Ruritania. It was an instant success.

Hope also wrote many other novels, historical romances, short stories and plays. Although his plays are now forgotten, he is still remembered for his two novels set in Ruritania, the second of which, *Rupert of Hentzau* (1898), follows the further adventures of Rudolf Rassendyll, the hero and narrator of *The Prisoner of Zenda.* Hope was knighted in 1918 for his services to his country.

In *The Prisoner of Zenda,* a burning curiosity draws Rudolf Rassendyll, a young Englishman, to Ruritania to see the coronation of the new king.

However, the king is kidnapped by his greedy and ambitious brother, the Duke of Strelsau, and only Rudolf can save him. He is thrown into a series of adventures beyond his wildest dreams and his own life is in danger as he tries to outwit the Duke and his evil henchmen, including the ruthless and fearless young Rupert Hentzau. At the same time he is deeply attracted to the beautiful and charming Princess Flavia, who is engaged to the king.

The Prisoner of Zenda has remained a popular novel for over a hundred years and the land of Ruritania has now taken its place on the map of English fiction and has inspired countless imitations in both literature and films.

1

"I wonder when in the world you are going to do anything, Rudolf?" asked my brother's wife.

"My dear Rose," I answered, "why in the world should I do anything? My position is a comfortable one. I have an income sufficient for my wants, I enjoy an enviable social position — I am brother to Lord Burlesdon, and brother-in-law to you, charming lady, his countess. Behold, it is enough!"

"You are nine-and-twenty," she observed, "and you've done nothing but...."

"Knock about? It is true. Our family does not need to do things."

This remark of mine rather annoyed Rose, for everybody knows that her family is not of the same standing as the Rassendylls. She possesses a large fortune, however, so my brother Robert is wise enough not to mind about her ancestry.

Robert came in and glanced at his wife's flushed cheeks.

"What's the matter, my dear?" he asked.

"She objects to my doing nothing," I observed in an injured tone.

"The difference between Robert and you," said my sister-in-law, "is that he recognises the duties of his position, and you see the opportunities of yours."

"To a man of spirit, my dear Rose," I answered, "opportunities are duties."

"Nonsense!" said she, tossing her head. After a moment or two she said, "Sir Jacob's offering you exactly what you might be equal to."

"A thousand thanks!" I murmured.

"He's to have an Embassy in six months, and Robert says he is sure that he'll take you as a special official. Do take it, Rudolf — to please me."

"My dear sister, if in six months' time Sir Jacob invites me, hang me if I don't go with him!"

"Oh, Rudolf, how good of you! I am glad!"

My promise, then, was given; but six months are six months, and seem an eternity. I looked around for some desirable way of spending them. And it occurred to me suddenly to visit Ruritania. It may seem strange that I had never visited that country, even though I was distantly related to the Elphbergs, who were the ruling family of Ruritania. My father had always been averse to my going, and since his death, my brother, prompted by Rose, had accepted the family tradition, which taught that a wide berth was to be given to that country. But the moment Ruritania came into my head I was eaten up with curiosity to see it. My decision was clinched when I read in *The Times* that Rudolf the Fifth was to be crowned at Strelsau in the course of the next three weeks, and that great magnificence was to mark the occasion. I at once made up my mind to be present, and began my preparations.

I informed my relatives that I was going for a ramble in the Tyrol — an old haunt of mine — and calmed Rose's wrath by declaring that I intended to study the political and social problems of the interesting community that dwells in the neighbourhood.

"Oh! You will write a book?" she cried, clapping her hands. "That would be splendid, wouldn't it, Robert?"

"It's the best introduction to political life nowadays," observed my brother.

"I believe you are right, Bob, my boy," said I.

"Now promise me you'll do it," said Rose earnestly.

"No, I will not promise, but if I find material enough, I will."

"That's fair enough," said Robert.

"Oh, material doesn't matter!" she said.

But she could not get anything more out of me. To tell the truth, I would have wagered a handsome sum that the story of my expedition that summer would stain no paper and spoil not a single pen. And that shows how little we know what the future holds; for here I am, fulfilling my promise, and writing, as I never thought to write, a book — though it will hardly serve as an introduction to political life, and has not a jot to do with the Tyrol.

Neither would it, I fear, please Lady Burlesdon if I were to submit it to her critical eye — a step that I have no intention of taking.

Even though she had pointed out the uselessness of my life, I had picked up a great deal of knowledge. I had been to a German university and spoke the language as readily and perfectly as English. I was thoroughly at home in French; I had a smattering of Italian and enough Spanish to swear by. I was, I believe, a strong, though hardly a fine swordsman and a good shot. I could ride anything that had a back to sit on; and my head was as cool as you could find. My parents had left me two thousand pounds a year and, with my roving disposition, I led a happy life.

2

It was my Uncle William's advice that no man should pass through Paris without spending four-and-twenty hours there. My uncle spoke out of a ripe experience of the world, and I honoured his advice by putting up for a day and night at 'The Continental' on my way to the Tyrol. I called on George Featherly at the Embassy, and after supper we visited Bertram Bertrand, a poet of some repute. We found him in low spirits. When I insisted on knowing the reason, he exclaimed, "I am in love."

"Oh, you'll write better poetry," said I, by way of consolation.

George said, "You might as well give her up. She's leaving Paris tomorrow."

"It would make it more interesting for me," I said, "if I knew who you were talking about."

"Antoinette de Mauban," replied George.

"Where's she going to?"

"Nobody knows," said George. "By the way, Bert, I met the Duke of Strelsau at her house the other night."

The lady was some sort of celebrity. She was a widow, rich and beautiful, and, according to some, ambitious. It is quite possible that she was interested in the duke, half-brother to the new King of Strelsau.

"He's not in Paris now, is he?" I asked.

"No. He's gone back to be present at the King's coronation, a ceremony which, I should say, he'll not enjoy much."

I was sorry for Bert and annoyed with George for causing him pain. So I returned to the hotel.

The next day George went with me to the station, where I took a ticket for Dresden.

"Going to see the pictures?" asked George, with a grin.

George is such a gossip that had I told him about my trip to Ruritania, the news would have been in London in three days and in Park Lane in a week. I was about to answer when, leaving me suddenly, he darted across the platform. Following him with my eyes, I saw him lift his hat to a graceful, fashionably dressed woman who had just appeared from the booking office. She was, perhaps, a year or two over thirty, tall, dark, and of rather full figure. As George talked, I saw her glance at me. A moment later, George returned.

"You've a charming travelling companion," he said. "That's Antoinette de Mauban, and like you, she's going to Dresden. It is queer, though, that she doesn't desire the honour of your acquaintance."

"I didn't ask to be introduced," I replied, a little annoyed.

When, after a night's rest in Dresden, I continued my journey, I observed that the lady got into the same train. Understanding that she wanted to be let alone, I avoided her, but saw that she went the same way as I did to the very end of my journey.

As soon as I reached the Ruritanian border, I bought a newspaper, and found in it news that made me change my travel plans. For some reason, the date of the King's coronation had been suddenly advanced, and the ceremony was to take place two days later.

Strelsau, I knew, was thronged with visitors who had come to watch the coronation ceremony. Rooms were all let and hotels overflowing; there would be very little chance of my obtaining any sort of lodging, and I certainly would have to pay an exorbitant charge for it. I made up my mind to stop at Zenda, a small town fifty miles short of the capital, and about ten from the border. My train reached there in the evening. I decided to spend the next day, Tuesday, wandering over the hills that were said to be very fine, and taking a look at the famous Castle. I would go over by train to Strelsau on Wednesday morning, returning at night to sleep at Zenda.

Accordingly I got out at Zenda, and as the train passed where I stood on the platform, I saw Madame Mauban in her place — clearly she was going through to Strelsau.

I was very kindly received at the hotel — it was more of an inn — kept by a fat old lady and her two daughters. They were good, quiet people, and seemed little interested in the coronation festivities in Strelsau. The old lady's hero was the duke, now master of the Zenda estates and of the Castle, which rose grandly on its steep hill at the end of the valley, a mile or so from the inn. The old lady did not hesitate to express regret that the duke was not on the throne, instead of his brother.

"We know Duke Michael," said she. "He has always lived with us; every Ruritanian knows him. But the King is almost a stranger. He lives abroad a great deal, not one in ten knows him even by sight."

"And now," chimed in one of the young women, "they say he has shaved off his beard, so that no one knows him at all. Johann, the duke's keeper, informed me that the King is at the duke's hunting-lodge, and will go from here to Strelsau to be crowned on Wednesday morning."

I was interested to hear this, and made up my mind to walk next day in the direction of the lodge, on the chance of coming across the King.

"This is the duke's land, you say. How, then, is the King here?" I asked.

"The duke invited him to rest here till Wednesday, whilst he is in Strelsau preparing the King's reception."

"Then they're friends?"

"Ay, they love one another as men who want the same place and the same wife!" put in the younger daughter.

The old woman looked at her angrily.

"What, the same wife, too! How's that, young lady?"

"All the world knows that the duke would give his soul to marry his cousin, Princess Flavia, and she is to be the queen."

"Upon my word," said I, "I begin to be sorry for your duke.'

"It's little dealing Black Michael, that is the duke, has with —" began the girl, braving her mother's anger; but as she spoke a heavy step sounded on the floor, and a gruff voice asked in a threatening tone:

"Who talks of 'Black Michael' in his Highness's own burgh?"

The girl gave a little shriek, half of fright — half, I think, of amusement.

'You'll not tell on me, Johann?" she said.

The man who had spoken came forward.

"We have company, Johann," said my hostess.

The fellow plucked off his hat. A moment later he saw me, and started back a step, as though he had seen something wonderful.

He soon recovered, and still staring at me, said, "Good evening to you, sir. I crave your pardon, sir. I expected to see no one."

"Good evening," I replied.

"It's the colour of your hair," one of the girls said, laughing. "It is a colour we do not see much in Zenda."

"Give him a glass to drink to my health and I shall bid you goodnight, and thank you, ladies, for your courtesy and pleasant conversation."

So speaking I rose to my feet, and with a slight bow, turned to the door. The young girl ran to light me on the way, and the man fell back to let me pass, his eyes still fixed on me. The moment I was by, he stepped forward and asked, "Pray, sir, do you know the King?"

"No," said I. "I hope to do so on Wednesday."

The girl, looking over her shoulder at me as she preceded me upstairs, said, "There's no pleasing Johann for one of your colour."

"What," asked I, "does colour matter in a man?"

"Nay, but I love yours — it's the Elphberg red."

"Colour in a man is of no importance to him," I replied.

In fact, however, as I now know, colour can sometimes be of considerable importance to a man.

3

Next morning, hearing that I was bound for Strelsau, Johann came to see me while I was breakfasting. He told me that his sister, who lived in the capital, had invited him to occupy a room in her house. He had gladly accepted, but now found that his duties would not permit his absence. He begged, therefore, that if such humble lodgings would satisfy me, I would take his place. He knew his sister would not mind, and said that he did not want me to suffer the inconvenience of travelling to and fro from Strelsau the next day. I accepted his offer without a moment's hesitation, and he went off to telegraph his sister.

I packed and prepared to take the next train. However, I still longed to explore the forest and see the hunting-lodge. When I was informed that the next roadside station was only about ten miles away, I decided to send my luggage directly from Zenda to the address that Johann had given, walk through the forest to the roadside station and follow to Strelsau myself. Johann had gone off and was not aware of the change in my plans.

I took an early luncheon and set out to climb the hill that led to the Castle, and thence to the forest of Zenda. Half an hour's walk brought me to the Castle. It had

once been a fortress, and was still in good condition. Behind it stood another portion of the original castle. Behind that again, and separated from it by a deep and broad moat, which ran all round the old buildings, was a modern chateau, erected by the last King, and now forming the country residence of the Duke of Strelsau. A drawbridge over the moat connected the old and the new castles, and this indirect mode of access formed the only passage between the old building and the outside world. Leading to the modern chateau was a broad and handsome avenue. It was an ideal residence. When 'Black Michael' did not desire company, he could simply have the drawbridge up, and nothing short of a regiment and a train of artillery could force him out. I went my way, glad that poor Black Michael, though he could not have the throne or the princess, had, at least, as fine a residence as any prince in Europe.

Soon I entered the forest, and walked on for an hour or more in its cool shade. I was enchanted with the place, and, finding a felled tree-trunk, propped my back against it. Then, stretching my legs out, I gave myself up to undisturbed contemplation of the beauty of the woods and the comfort of a good cigar. When the cigar was finished and I had taken in as much beauty as I could, I fell into the most delightful sleep, regardless of my train to Strelsau.

Suddenly I thought I heard someone exclaim, "Why, the devil's in it! Shave him, and he'd be the King!"

I opened my eyes, and found two men regarding me with much curiosity. Both wore shooting costumes and carried guns. One was rather short and very stoutly built, with a big bullet-shaped head, a bristly grey moustache, and small pale-blue eyes. The other was a slender young fellow, of middle height, and dark in complexion. I set one down as an old soldier, and the other for a gentleman accustomed to good society, but not unused to military life either.

The elder man approached me, while the younger followed and courteously raised his hat. I rose slowly to my feet.

"He's the height, too!" I heard the elder murmur, as he surveyed my height of six feet two inches. "May I ask your name, sir?"

"As you have taken the first step in the acquaintance, gentlemen," said I, with a smile, "suppose you give me a lead in the matter of names."

The young man stepped forward with a pleasant smile.

"This," he said, "is Colonel Sapt, and I am called Fritz von Tarlenheim: we are both in the service of the King of Ruritania."

I bowed, and taking off my hat, said, "I am Rudolf Rassendyll. I am a traveller from England; and once, for a year or two, I held a commission from her Majesty the Queen."

"Then we are all brethren of the sword," answered Fritz, holding out his hand, which I took readily.

"Rassendyll, Rassendyll!" muttered Sapt; then a gleam of intelligence flitted across his face.

"By Heaven!" he cried, " you're of the Burlesdons?"

"My brother is now Lord Burlesdon," said I.

"The hair betrays you," he chuckled. "Why, Fritz, you know the story?"

The young man looked embarrassed. To put him at his ease, I remarked with a smile, "The scandal is known here as well as among us, it seems. Many years ago, a certain Burlesdon lady had an affair with an Elphberg. Since then, the red hair of the Elphbergs appears once in a few generations among the Burlesdons."

At this moment a ringing voice sounded from the wood behind us:

"Fritz! Fritz! Where are you, man?"

Fritz started, and said hastily:

"It's the King!"

A young man jumped out from behind the trunk of a tree and stood beside us. As I looked at him, I uttered an astonished cry; and he, seeing me, drew back in sudden wonder. But for the hair on my face and a manner of conscious dignity which his position gave him, the King of Ruritania might have been Rudolf Rassendyll, and I, Rudolf, the King.

For a moment we stood motionless, looking at one another. Then I bared my head, and bowed respectfully. The King found his voice and asked, "Colonel — Fritz — who is this gentleman?"

I was about to answer, when Colonel Sapt stepped between us and began to talk to his Majesty. The King towered over Sapt, and, as he listened, his eyes now and again sought mine. I looked at him long and carefully. The likeness was certainly astonishing.

Sapt ceased speaking, and the King still frowned. Then, gradually, the corners of his mouth began to twitch, his eyes twinkled and he burst into the merriest of laughter, which rang through the woods and proclaimed him a jovial soul.

"Well met, cousin!" he cried.

He stepped up to me, and clapped me on the back, still laughing.

"You must forgive me if I was taken aback. A man doesn't expect to see double at this time of the day, eh, Fritz?" Then turning to me, he asked, "Where are you travelling to?"

"To Strelsau, sire — to the coronation."

The King looked at his friends.

"Fritz, Fritz!" he cried, "a thousand crowns for a sight of brother Michael's face when he sees a pair of us!" and the merry laugh rang out again.

"Seriously," observed Fritz, "I question Mr Rassendyll's wisdom in visiting Strelsau just now."

The King lit a cigarette.

"Well, Sapt?" said he, questioningly.

"He mustn't go," growled the old fellow.

"Come, colonel, you mean that I should be in Mr. Rassendyll's debt, if—"

"Oh yes! Put it as politely as you wish," said Sapt.

"Enough, sire," said I. "I'll leave Ruritania today."

"No, by thunder, you shan't. For you shall dine with me tonight, come what may afterwards. Come, man, you don't meet a new relation every day. By the way, what name did they give you?"

"Your Majesty's," I answered.

"Come, then, cousin Rudolf and we'll entertain you in my dear brother's hunting lodge."

We walked for more than half an hour, and the King smoked and chatted incessantly. He was full of interest in my family, and laughed heartily when he heard that my trip to Ruritania was a secret one.

Emerging from the woods, we came upon a small hunting-lodge. It was a single-storey building, made entirely of wood. As we approached it, a bearded man in a plain livery came out to meet us. The only other person I saw about the place was a fat elderly lady. She was Johann's mother.

"Well, is dinner ready, Josef?" asked the King.

The servant informed us that it was, and we soon sat down to a plentiful meal. The King ate heartily, Fritz delicately and old Sapt voraciously. The King called for wine to be served.

"Remember tomorrow!" Fritz cautioned him.

"Ay — tomorrow!" growled old Sapt.

The wine was beyond all price and praise, and we did it justice. Fritz ventured once to stay the King's hand.

"What?" cried the King. "Remember you start before I do, Master Fritz — you must be more sparing than I."

"The colonel and I," explained Fritz to me, "will leave early for Zenda, and return with the guard of honour to fetch the king."

At last the King set down his glass and leant back in his chair.

"I have drunk enough," he said.

Just then Josef came and set an old wicker-covered flagon before him.

"His Highness the Duke of Strelsau bade me, sire," said Josef, "that when the King was weary of all other wines, to set this wine before the King, and pray the King to drink, for the love that he bears his brother."

"Well done, Black Michael!" said the King. "Out with the cork, Josef. Did he think I'd flinch from his bottle?"

The bottle was opened, and Josef filled the King's glass. The King tasted it, then seized the bottle and turned it over his mouth. He drained the flagon, flung it from him, and laid his head on his arms on the table.

Wishing him pleasant dreams, we drank some more, and that is all I remember of the evening.

4

I awoke with a start, dripping wet. Old Sapt stood opposite me, an empty bucket in his hand. On the table by him sat Fritz.

I leapt to my feet in anger.

"Your joke goes too far, sir!" I cried.

"We've no time for quarrelling, man. Nothing else would rouse you. It's five o'clock."

I looked angrily at them, feeling uncommonly cold.

"Rassendyll," said Fritz, getting down from the table and taking my arm, "look here."

The King lay full length on the floor, breathing heavily. Sapt, the disrespectful man, kicked him sharply. He did not stir. I saw his face and head were wet with water, as were mine.

"We've spent half an hour on him," said Fritz.

"Was the wine drugged — the last bottle?" I asked.

"I don't know," said Sapt. "The way he is, he'll not move for six or seven hours yet."

"But the coronation!" I cried in horror.

Fritz shrugged his shoulders.

"We must send word that he is ill," he said.

"If he's not crowned today," said old Sapt, puffing away at his pipe, "I'll bet a crown he'll never be crowned."

"But heavens, why?"

"The whole nation's there to meet him; half the army — and Black Michael at the head. Shall we send word that the King is drunk?"

"That he is ill," said I, in correction.

Sapt raised his hand.

"Do you think the wine was drugged?"

"I do," said I.

"And who drugged it?"

"That hound, Black Michael," said Fritz between his teeth.

"Ay, that he might not come to be crowned. The throne is lost if the King does not show himself in Strelsau today. I know Black Michael."

"We could carry him there," said I.

Sapt stirred him again with his foot.

"The drunken dog!" he said. "But he is his father's son, and an Elphberg, after all. May I rot in hell before Black Michael sits in his place!"

For a moment or two we were all silent; then Sapt took his pipe from his mouth and said to me:

"As a man grows old, he believes in Fate. Fate sent you here. Fate sends you now to Strelsau."

I staggered back, murmuring, "Good God!"

Fritz looked up with an eager, bewildered gaze.

"Impossible!" I muttered. "I should be known."

"It's a risk, I'll acknowledge that," said Sapt. "But if you shave, I'll bet that you will not be known. Are you afraid?"

"Sir!"

"I know it is dangerous. But if you don't go, I swear to you Black Michael will sit tonight on the throne, and the King will lie in prison or his grave."

"The King will never forgive it," I stammered.

"Who cares for his forgiveness?"

The clock ticked away as I stood in thought. Then I suppose a look came over my face, for old Sapt caught me by the hand, crying, "You'll go?"

"Yes, I'll go," said I, and turned my eyes on the figure of the King on the floor.

"Tonight," Sapt went on in a hasty whisper, "we are to lodge in the Palace. The moment they leave us, you and I will mount our horses — Fritz must stay and guard the King's room — and ride here at a gallop. The King will be ready — Josef will tell him — and he must ride back with me to Strelsau, and you ride as if the devil were behind you to the border."

I took it all in quickly, and nodded my head.

"There's a chance," said Fritz, with the first sign of hopefulness.

"If I escape detection," said I.

"If we are detected," said Sapt, "I'll send Black Michael down before I go myself, so help me heaven! Sit in that chair, man."

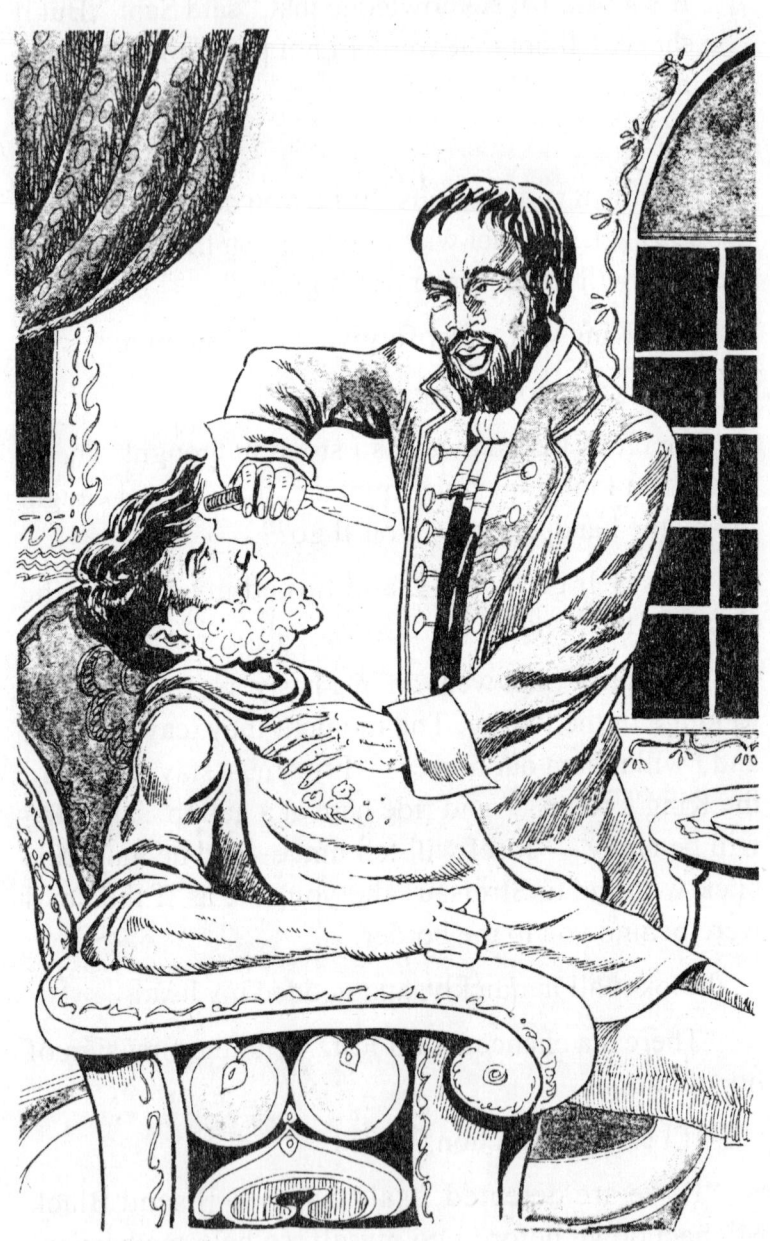

I obeyed him.

He darted from the room, calling, "Josef! Josef!"

In three minutes he was back, and Josef with him, carrying a jug of hot water, soap and razors. Sapt bade him shave me.

Suddenly Fritz smote his thigh.

"But the guard! They'll know! They'll know!"

"Pooh! We shan't wait for the guard. We'll ride to Hofbau and catch a train there. When they come, the bird'll have flown."

"But the King?"

"The King will be in the wine-cellar. I'm going to carry him there now."

"If they find him?"

"They won't. How should they? Josef will put them off."

"But...."

Sapt stamped his foot.

"We're not playing," he roared. "My God! Don't I know the risk?"

So speaking, he lifted the King and bore him off in his arms. As he did so, we saw Johann's mother standing in the doorway. She stood there for a moment, then turned, and without a sign of surprise, clattered down the passage.

"Has she heard?" cried Fritz.

"I'll shut her mouth!" said Sapt grimly, as he went down to the wine-cellar.

I sat down in an armchair, half-dazed. Josef clipped and scraped me till my face was as bare as the King's. And when Fritz saw me thus, he drew a long breath and exclaimed:

"By Jove, we shall do it!"

It was six o'clock now, and we had no time to lose. Sapt hurried me to the King's room, and I dressed myself in the uniform of a colonel of the Guard, finding time as I slipped on the King's boots, to ask Sapt what he had done with the old woman.

"She swore she'd heard nothing," said he, "but to make sure, I tied her legs together and put a handkerchief in her mouth and bound her hands, and locked her up in the coal-cellar, next door to the King. Josef will look after them both later on."

I burst out laughing, and even old Sapt grimly smiled.

I put the King's helmet on my head. Sapt handed me the King's sword, looking at me long and carefully.

"Thank God Josef shaved off your beard!" he exclaimed.

Fritz now rejoined us in the uniform of a captain in the same regiment as that to which my dress belonged. In four minutes Sapt had arrayed himself in his uniform. When Josef brought the horses, we mounted and started off at a rapid trot. The game had begun.

On the way, Sapt filled me in with details about the past life of the King, his habits, friends and servants.

When we arrived at the station, Fritz explained to the astonished stationmaster that the King had changed his plans. We got into the first class compartment. I looked at my watch — the King's watch, I mean. It was eight o'clock.

At half-past nine, I saw the towers and spires of a great city.

"Your capital, my King," said old Sapt with a smile. "We're an hour early. We'll send word of the King's arrival. And meanwhile —"

"Meanwhile," said I, "the King will be hanged if he doesn't have some breakfast."

Old Sapt chuckled, and held out his hand, saying, "You're an Elphberg, every inch of you. Pray that we may be alive tonight."

The train stopped. Fritz and Sapt leapt out, and held the door for me. I choked down a lump that rose in my throat, settled my helmet firmly on my head, and breathed a short prayer to God. Then I stepped on the platform of the station.

A moment later, all was bustle and confusion. People rushed to greet me, some of them hurried me to the buffet, the bells throughout the city broke out into a joyful peal, and the sound of a military band and of men cheering reached us.

King Rudolf the Fifth was in his good city of Strelsau! And they shouted outside:

"God save the King!"

Old Sapt's mouth wrinkled into a smile.

"God save them both!" he whispered. "Courage, lad!"

5

With Fritz and Sapt close behind me, I stepped out of the buffet on to the platform. The last thing I did was to feel if my revolver and sword were handy. A group of soldiers and high dignitaries awaited me. Sapt stood behind, whispering into my ear the names of the two men who greeted me — Marshal Strakencz, the most famous veteran of the Ruritanian army, and the Chancellor of the Kingdom.

The duke, it seemed, had been taken ill and would await His Majesty at the Cathedral. I expressed my concern, accepted the Marshal's excuses very graciously, and received the compliments of a large number of distinguished personages. No one betrayed the least suspicion, and I felt my nerve returning.

Presently we formed a procession and made our way to the door of the station. Here I mounted my horse and started to ride through the streets, with the Marshal on my right and Sapt on my left. The scene was very brilliant as we passed along the Grand Boulevard and on to the great square where the Royal Palace stood. Here I was in the midst of my devoted subjects. Every house was hung with red and bedecked with flags. The streets were lined with raised seats on each side, and I passed along, bowing this way and that, under showers of cheers, blessings, and waving handkerchiefs.

I was drunk with excitement. At that moment I believed — I almost believed — that I was the King. I looked up laughing, at the balconies thronged with beautiful ladies. And then I started. For, looking down on me was Antoinette de Mauban; and I saw her start too, and her lips moved, and she leant forward and gazed at me. But, collecting myself, I met her eyes full and square.

We moved on. At last we were at the Cathedral. Everything was in a mist as I dismounted. My eyes were still dim as I walked up the great steps, with the pealing of the organ in my ears. I saw nothing of the brilliant throng around me. Two faces stood out side by side clearly before my eyes. One was the face of a girl, pale and lovely, surmounted by a crown of the glorious Elphberg red hair; the second was the face of a man, whose black hair and deep eyes told me that at last I was in the presence of my brother, Black Michael. When he saw me, his red cheeks went pale and his helmet fell with a clatter on the floor. Till that moment, I believe he had not realised that the King was really in Strelsau.

I remember nothing of what followed. I knelt at the altar and the Cardinal anointed my head. Then I rose to my feet, stretched out my hand and took the crown of Ruritania from him and set it on my head, and I swore the oath of the King. After this, I received the Holy Sacrament before them all, and the great organ pealed out again. The Marshal bade the heralds proclaim me, and Rudolf the Fifth was crowned King.

Then the lady with the pale face and the glorious hair stepped from her place and came to where I stood. And a herald cried:

"Her Royal Highness, the Princess Flavia!"

She curtsied low, and putting her hand under mine, raised my hand and kissed it. For an instant I wondered what it was that I had to do. Then I drew her to me and kissed her twice on the cheek. The Cardinal Archbishop slipped in front of Black Michael, kissed my hand and presented me a letter from the Pope.

And then came the Duke of Strelsau. His steps trembled, I swear, and he looked to the right and to the left. His face was patched with red and white, and his hand shook so that it jumped under mine, and I felt his lips dry. I took Michael with both my hands and kissed him on the cheek. I think we were both glad when that was over.

All this while, neither in the face of the princess nor in that of any other, did I see the least doubt or questioning. So the likeness served, and for an hour I stood there while everybody kissed my hand, and the ambassadors paid their respects.

Then we went back through the streets to the palace. I was now in a carriage, side by side with the Princess Flavia.

"Rudolf, you look different today," said she.

The fact was not surprising, but the remark was disquieting.

"It must be the reception," I said. "I assure you, my dear cousin, that nothing in my life has affected me more than the reception I've been greeted with today."

She smiled brightly, but in an instant grew grave again, and whispered, "Did you notice Michael?"

"Yes," said I, adding, "he wasn't enjoying himself."

"Do be careful!" she went on.

We had reached the Palace. Guns were firing and trumpets blowing. The princess and I went up the broad marble staircase. and then I took formal possession, as a crowned King, of the House of my ancestors, and sat down at my table. Soon my cousin joined me and sat on my right. On her other side sat Black Michael, and on my left the Cardinal. Behind my chair stood Sapt, and at the end of the table I saw Fritz.

I wondered what the King of Ruritania was doing.

6

We were in the King's dressing room—Fritz, Sapt and I.

"What a day for you to remember!" Fritz cried. "But Rassendyll, you mustn't throw your heart too much into the part. Did you see Black Michael look blacker thar ever? You and the princess had so much to say to one another."

"How beautiful she is!" I exclaimed.

"Never mind her," growled Sapt. "Are you ready to start?"

"Yes,' said I, with a sigh.

It was five o'clock, and at twelve I should be no more than Rudolf Rassendyll.

Sapt said grimly, "Do you know, friend, that Michael has had news from Zenda? He went into a room alone to read it — and he came out looking dazed."

"I'm ready," said I, this news making me eager to leave.

"Now, Fritz," said Sapt, "the King goes to bed. He is upset. No one is to see him till nine o'clock tomorrow. You understand — no one."

"I understand," answered Fritz.

"Michael may come, so we have to take precautions. Here, wrap yourself in this big cloak and put on this flat cap. My orderly, that's you, rides with me to the hunting-lodge."

Fritz held out his hand.

"In case," said he; and we shook hands heartily.

"Come along," growled Sapt.

I followed him. We walked about two hundred yards along a narrow passage till we came to a stout oak door. Sapt unlocked it. Outside we found a man waiting with two horses. Without a word, we mounted and rode away. The town was full of noise and merriment, but we took secluded ways. At last we came to the city wall and to a gate.

"Have your weapon ready," whispered Sapt. "We must stop the guard's mouth if he talks."

A little girl of fourteen tripped out.

"Please, sirs, my father has gone to see the King. But he said I wasn't to open the gate."

"Did he, my dear?" said Sapt, dismounting. "Then I will open it. Give me the key."

Sapt gave her a crown and an order from the King that he had forged, and said, "Here's an order from the King. Show it to your father. Orderly, open the gate!"

I, now an orderly, leapt down and between us, we rolled back the gate, and closed it again after leading our horses out.

Once outside the town, we quickened our pace. We stopped for a draught of wine and to rest the horses, thus losing half an hour. Then we rode on again, and had covered some twenty-five miles when Sapt abruptly stopped.

"Hark!" he cried.

I listened. Away, far behind us, we heard the beat of horses' hooves. I glanced at Sapt.

"Come on!" he cried, and spurred his horse into a gallop. When we next paused to listen, the hoof-beats were not audible, and we relaxed our pace. Then we heard them again. Sapt jumped down and laid his ear to the ground.

"There are two," he said. "They're only a mile behind."

We galloped on. Another half an hour brought us to a divide in the road. Sapt drew rein.

"Get down," he said.

"But they'll be on us!" I cried.

"Get down!" he repeated and I obeyed. The wood was dense up to the very edge of the road. We led our horses into the wood, bound handkerchiefs over their eyes, and stood beside them.

Nearer and nearer came the hooves. The moon shone out clear and full.

"It's the duke!" I whispered.

"I thought so," he answered.

It was the duke and with him, a burly fellow — brother of Johann, the keeper.

"Which way?" asked Black Michael.

"To the Castle, your Highness," urged his companion. "There we shall learn the truth."

The duke hesitated for a moment.

"I thought I heard hooves," said he.

"I think not, your Highness."

"Why shouldn't we go to the lodge?"

"I fear a trap. If all is well, why go to the lodge? If not, it's a snare to trap us."

Suddenly the duke's horse neighed. In an instant, we folded our cloaks round our horses' heads, and, holding them thus, covered the duke and his attendant with our revolvers. If they had found us, they would have been dead men, or our prisoners.

Michael waited a moment longer. Then he cried:

"To Zenda, then!" and setting spurs to his horse, galloped on.

We stayed where we were for ten minutes. Then we mounted, and rode towards the lodge as fast as our weary horses could take us. At last the lodge came in sight. Spurring our horses, we rode past the gate. All was still and quiet. Suddenly Sapt caught my arm and pointed to the ground.

"Look there!"

I looked down. At my feet lay five or six silk handkerchiefs, torn and slashed and rent. I turned to him questioningly.

"These are what I tied the old woman with," said he. "Fasten the horses and come along."

We rushed down the passage towards the cellars. The door of the coal-cellar stood wide open.

"They found the old woman," said I.

We came to the door of the wine-cellar. It was shut. It looked in all respects as it had looked when we left it that morning.

A loud oath from Sapt rang out. His face turned pale, and he pointed again to the floor. From under the door a red stain had spread over the floor of the passage and dried there. Sapt sank against the wall. I tried the door. It was locked.

In my terror and excitement, I rained blows on the lock of the door, and fired a cartridge into it. It gave way and the door swung open. I went and took a silver candlestick from the dining table and struck a light. I walked into the cellar and held the candle high above my head. I saw the body of a man, lying flat on his back, a crimson gash across his throat. It was the body of Josef, the faithful servant, slain while guarding the King.

I felt a hand on my shoulders, and, turning, saw Sapt, eyes glaring and terror-struck, beside me.

"The King! My God, the King!" he whispered hoarsely.

I threw the candle's gleam over every inch of the cellar.

"The King is not here," I said.

7

"They've got the King!" shouted Sapt.

"Yes," said I. "We must get back to Strelsau and rouse every soldier. We ought to be in pursuit of Michael before midday."

"Who knows where the King is now?" he asked. He sat still, thinking for a while.

Then he burst into one of his chuckles and said, "Ay, lad, we'll go back to Strelsau. The King shall be in his capital tomorrow."

"The King?"

"The crowned King!"

"You're mad!" I cried.

He rose, came to me and laid his hand on my shoulder.

"Lad," he said, "if you play the man, you may save the King yet. Go back and keep his throne warm for him."

"But the duke and his men know —"

"Ay, but they can't speak!" roared Sapt. "How can they denounce you without denouncing themselves? 'This is not the King, because we have kidnapped the King and murdered his servant.' Can they say that?"

I knew what Sapt was trying to say, but I saw the difficulties.

"I will be found out," I urged.

"Perhaps, but every hour counts. Above all we must have a King in Strelsau, or the city will be Michael's in twenty-four hours, and what would the King's life be worth then — or his throne? Lad, you must do it!"

"Suppose they kill the King?"

"They'll kill him, if you don't sit on that throne."

It was a wild plan — and even more hopeless than the trick we had already carried through; but as I listened to Sapt I saw the strong points in our game.

"Sapt," I cried, "I'll try it!"

"Well played!" said he.

I insisted on giving Josef a decent burial, but before I could do so, Sapt drew me to the door and pointed. Coming along the road from Zenda, I made out a party of men — four were on horseback, the rest were walking. They all carried long implements on their shoulders.

"There's no time. Come along," Sapt said.

We retreated through the house and made our way to the back entrance. Here we mounted our horses, drew our swords, and waited silently. After a minute or two, we heard the tramp of men on the other side of the house. They came to a stand, and one cried out:

"Now then. Fetch him out!"

"Now!" whispered Sapt.

Driving the spurs into our horses, we rushed round the house, and in a moment we were among the ruffians. Raising my sword, I split the head of a fellow on a brown horse, and he fell to the ground. Then I found myself opposite a big man, and was conscious of another to my right. With a simultaneous action, I drove my spurs into my horse again and my sword slashed into the big man's breast. I tried to wrench the sword out, but could not. I dropped it and galloped after Sapt.

We rode on in gloomy silence. The day broke clear and cold. We kept up our pace till Strelsau lay before us. The streets were quiet; everyone was sleeping off last night's revelry. We hardly met a soul till we reached the little gate of the Palace. Sapt's old groom was waiting for us.

"Is all well, sir?" he asked.

"All's well," said Sapt, and the man, coming to me, took my hand to kiss.

We went in and reached the dressing room. Flinging open the door, we saw Fritz stretched, fully dressed, on the sofa. Our entry woke him and he leapt to his feet. He gave one glance at me, and with a joyful cry, threw himself on his knees before me.

"Thank God, sire! Thank God you're safe!" he cried, stretching his hand to catch mine.

I confess I was moved. The King, whatever his faults, made people love him. For a moment I could not speak or bear to break the poor fellow's illusion. But tough old Sapt had no such feeling. He slapped his hand on his thigh delightedly.

"Bravo, lad!" he cried. "We shall do it yet!"

Fritz looked up in bewilderment. He rose to his feet slowly. Then he looked me up and down and suddenly dropped my hand.

"Where's the King? Where's the King?" he cried.

"Hush, you fool!" hissed Sapt. "Not so loud! Here's the King!"

A knock sounded at the door. Sapt seized me by the hand.

"Quick, to the bedroom! Off with your cap and boots. Get into bed. Cover everything up."

I did as I was bid. A moment later Sapt looked in, nodded, and introduced a young man, who came up to my bedside, bowing again and again. He informed me that Her Royal Highness, the Princess Flavia, had sent him especially to enquire after the King's health.

"My best thanks, sir, to my cousin," said I. "Tell her Royal Highness that I was never better in my life."

"The King," added Sapt, "has slept without a break all night."

The young gentleman bowed himself out. Fritz's pale face brought us back to reality.

"Is the King dead?" he whispered.

"Please God, no," said I. "But he is in the hands of Black Michael!"

8

A real king's life is perhaps a hard one, but a pretended king's is, I warrant, much harder. The next day, Sapt instructed me in my duties — what I ought to do and what I ought to know — for three hours. Then I snatched breakfast, with Sapt still opposite me, telling me that the King always took white wine in the morning and was known to desist from all highly seasoned dishes. Then came the Chancellor, for another three hours, and after him the French ambassador was introduced, to present his credentials. Then, at last, I was left alone. I told Sapt that I was tired and would like to rest.

Fritz, who was standing by, cried, "By Heaven! We waste time. Aren't we going to throw Black Michael by the heels?"

"Do you think Michael will fall and leave the King alive?" asked Sapt.

"And," I suggested, "while the King is here in Strelsau, on his throne, what grievance has he against his dear brother Michael?"

"Are we to do nothing, then?"

"We're to do nothing stupid," growled Sapt.

"But he'll kill the King," insisted Fritz.

"Not he," said Sapt.

"Half of the Six are in Strelsau," said Fritz.

"Only half? You're sure?" Sapt asked eagerly.

"Yes — only half."

"Then the King is alive, for the other three are guarding him!" cried Sapt.

"Who are the Six?" I asked, as I did not know whom they were talking about.

"They are six gentlemen who belong to Michael body and soul."

"They'd all cut a throat if Michael told them to," said Fritz.

"Perhaps they'll cut mine," I suggested. "What are their names?"

"The ones who are here," said Fritz, "are De Gautet, Bersonin, and Detchard."

I wondered what my future course of action should be.

I decided, then and there, to make myself as popular as I could, and at the same time, not show any disfavour to Michael. I had a fine game to play in Strelsau. Michael should not grow stronger for delay.

I ordered my horse, and, attended by Fritz, rode in the grand avenue of the Royal Park, returning all the salutes with politeness. Then I rode through a few streets, bought flowers of a pretty girl and rode to the residence of the Princess Flavia, and asked if she would receive me.

She received me very well.

"You are gaining laurels," she said. "You are like the prince in Shakespeare who was transformed by becoming king. But I am forgetting that you are the King, sire."

"I ask you to speak nothing but what your heart tells you — and to call me by my name."

She looked at me for a moment.

"Then I'm glad and proud, Rudolf," she said. "Why, as I told you, your very face has changed."

Wishing to change the topic, I said, "My brother is back, I hear. He made an excursion, didn't he?"

"Yes, he's here," she said, frowning a little.

"You don't care for Michael?"

"Ah, cousin Michael! I refer to him as the Duke of Strelsau, but I call him Michael when I meet him, by your father's orders."

"And now by mine?"

"If those are your orders."

"Oh, decidedly! We must all be pleasant to our dear Michael."

As I spoke, there came a cheer from the street. The princess ran to the window.

"It is he!" she cried. "It is — the Duke of Strelsau!"

I smiled, but said nothing. Soon I heard the tread of feet in the ante-room. I had begun to talk to Flavia on general matters, when all of a sudden, clasping her hands, she asked in an agitated voice:

"Are you wise to make him angry?"

"What? Who? How can I make him angry?"

"By keeping him waiting."

"I don't want to keep him waiting."

"How funny you are," she said. "You know very well that no one can be announced while I am with you."

"An excellent etiquette!" I cried. "But I had clean forgotten it."

I jumped up, flung the door open, and went into the ante-room. Michael was sitting at a table, a heavy frown on his face.

I held out my hand. Michael took it, and I embraced him. Then I drew him into the inner room.

"Brother," I said, "if I had known you were here, you would not have waited a moment."

He thanked me, but coldly. The man had many qualities, but he could not hide his feelings. A mere stranger could have seen that he hated me, and hated worse to see me with Princess Flavia.

I began to compliment him on the magnificent condition of his regiment, and of their loyal greeting to me on the day of my coronation. Thence I passed to a rapturous description of the hunting-lodge he had lent me. But he suddenly rose to his feet. His temper was failing him, and, with an excuse, he said farewell. However, as he reached the door, he stopped, saying:

"Three friends of mine are very anxious to have the honour of being presented to you, sire. They are here in the ante-chamber."

I joined him directly, passing my arm through his. We entered the ante-chamber in fraternal fashion. Michael beckoned, and three men came forward.

"These gentlemen," said Michael, with a stately courtesy that he could assume with perfect grace and ease, "are the most loyal and the most devoted of your Majesty's servants, and are my very faithful and dearest friends."

"I am very pleased to meet them," said I.

They came one by one and kissed my hand — De Gautet, a tall lean fellow; Bersonin, the Belgian, a portly man of middle height with a bald head; and last, the Englishman, Detchard, a narrow-faced fellow. He was a finely-made man, broad at the shoulder. I put him down for a good fighter, but a crooked customer.

Having got rid of my brother and his friends, I returned to take leave of my cousin.

"Rudolf," she said, very low, "be careful, won't you?"

"Of what?"

"You know — I can't say. But think what your life is to...."

"Well, to...?"

"To Ruritania."

"Only to Ruritania?" I asked softly.

"And to your cousin," she whispered, "and loving servant."

I could not speak. I kissed her hand, and went out.

9

One day Sapt came into my room. He threw me a letter, saying:

"That's for you — a woman's hand, I think. But I have some news for you first."

"What is it?"

"The King's at the Castle of Zenda."

"How do you know?"

"Because the other half of Michael's Six are there — Lauengram, Krafstein, and young Rupert Hentzau — three rogues."

"Well?"

"Fritz wants you to march to the Castle with horse, foot and artillery."

"Then I'll go to Zenda," I said.

"You're mad," said Sapt.

"I can take care of myself."

"De Gautet, Bersonin and Detchard are in Strelsau; and any one of them, lad, would cut your throat readily—as readily as I would Black Michael's. What's the letter?"

I opened it and read it aloud:

If the King desires to know what deeply concerns him, let him do as this letter bids him. At the end of the New Avenue stands a house. It has a portico, with a statue of a nymph on it. A wall encloses the garden; there is a gate in the wall at the back. At twelve o'clock tonight, if the King enters alone by the gate, turns to the right, and walks twenty yards, he will find a summerhouse, approached by a flight of six steps. If he mounts and enters, he will find someone who will tell him what touches his life and his throne most dearly. Please believe a faithful friend. He must be alone. If he neglects this invitation, his life will be in danger. He must not show this letter to anyone, or he will ruin a woman who loves Black Michael, and Black Michael does not pardon.

"No," observed Sapt, as I ended, "but he can dictate a very pretty letter."

"Hallo! There's some more!"

If you hesitate, consult Colonel Sapt. Ask him what woman would do most to prevent the duke from marrying his cousin, and therefore most to prevent him becoming King? And ask him if her name begins with — A?

I sprang to my feet.

"Antoinette de Mauban, by heaven!" I cried.

"How do you know?"

I told him what I knew of the lady, and how I knew it. He nodded.

"I shall go, Sapt."

"No, I shall go," said he.

"Sapt, I believe in that woman, and I shall go."

"I don't believe in any woman," said Sapt, "and you shan't go."

"I either go to the summerhouse or back to England," said I. "Time is running out, Sapt. We must force the game."

"So be it," he said, with a sigh.

To cut the story short, at half-past eleven Sapt and I mounted our horses. Fritz was again left on guard, our destination not being revealed to him. It was a very dark night. I carried a revolver, a long knife, and a bull's-eye lantern. We arrived outside the gate. I dismounted. Sapt held out his hand.

"I shall wait here," he said. "If I hear a shot, I'll...."

"Stay where you are; it is the King's only chance. Nothing should happen to you."

I opened the gate and found myself in a sort of wild shrubbery. I cautiously followed the instructions given in the letter. I mounted the steps of the summerhouse and opened the door. A woman flew to me and seized my hand.

"Shut the door," she whispered.

I obeyed. The summerhouse was a bare little room, furnished only with a couple of chairs and a small iron table. The woman was in an evening dress.

"Don't talk," she said. "We have no time. Listen! I know you, Mr Rassendyll. I wrote that letter at the duke's orders. In twenty minutes three men will be here to kill you."

"*The* three?"

"Yes. You must be gone by then. If not, you'll be killed."

"Or they will."

"Listen! Listen! They will murder the King in the Castle and the duke will proclaim either himself or the princess as the new ruler — himself, if he is strong enough. Anyhow, he'll marry her, and become king in fact, and soon in name. Do you see?"

"It's a pretty plot. But why, madame, do you...?"

"Say I'm a Christian — or say I'm jealous. Shall I see him marry her? Now go; but remember — this is what I have to tell you — that never, by night or by day, are you safe. Three men follow you. They're never more than two hundred yards from you. Your life is not worth a moment if ever they find you alone. Now go softly, past the summerhouse for a hundred yards, and you'll find a ladder against the wall. Go over it and fly for your life."

"And you?"

"I have my game to play too. If Michael finds out what I have done, we shall not meet again. If not, we may yet. Go at once."

I took her hand and kissed it.

"Madame," said I, "you have served the King well tonight. Where is he in the Castle?"

She sank her voice to a fearful whisper.

"Across the drawbridge is a heavy door. Behind that lies — Hark! What's that?"

Footsteps sounded outside.

"They're coming! They're too soon!" And she turned pale as death.

I cocked my revolver. A voice came from outside.

"Mr Rassendyll, we want to talk to you."

I made no answer.

"Will you promise not to shoot till we've done?" the voice asked.

"Have I the pleasure of addressing Mr Detchard?" I said.

"Never mind the names."

"Then let mine alone."

"All right, sire. I've an offer for you. Will you let us in? We pledge our honour to observe the truce."

"Don't trust them," whispered Antoinette.

"We can speak through the door," said I. "I give you my word of honour not to fire before you do, but I won't let you in. Stand outside and talk. What's the offer?"

"A safe conduct to the border, and fifty thousand pounds English."

"Give me a minute to consider," I said. I thought I heard a laugh outside.

I turned to Antoinette.

"Stand close to the wall, out of the line of fire from the door," I whispered to her.

I took up the iron table and held it by the legs. The top, protruding in front of me, made a complete screen for my head and body. I fastened the closed lantern to my belt and put my revolver in a handy pocket. Suddenly I saw the door move ever so slightly.

I drew back as far as I could from the door, holding the table in front of me. Then I called out.

"Gentlemen, I accept your offer, relying on your honour. If you will please open the door...."

"Open it yourself," said Detchard.

"It opens outward," said I. "Stand back."

I went and fumbled with the latch, and stole back to my place on tiptoe.

"I can't open it!" I cried. "The latch is caught."

"I'll open it!" cried Detchard.

An instant later the door was flung back. The gleam of a lantern showed me three men close together outside, their revolvers levelled. With a shout, I charged across the summerhouse and through the doorway. Three shots rang out, and battered into my shield. In another moment, I leapt out and the table caught the men full and square, and in a tumbling, swearing, struggling mass, they and I and the brave table, rolled down the steps of the summerhouse to the ground below. Antoinette shrieked, but I rose to my feet, laughing.

De Gautet and Bersonin lay like men stunned. Detchard was under the table, but as I rose, he pushed it from him and fired again. I raised my revolver and took a shot at him. I heard him curse, and then I ran like a hare, laughing as I went, past the summerhouse and along by the wall. I heard steps behind me. I turned and fired again. The steps ceased.

I found the ladder and was up and over it in a minute. I saw the horses, and then I saw Sapt. He had heard us, and was battling with the locked gate. I clapped him on the shoulder and said, "Come home to bed, old chap."

He started and cried, "You're safe!" and wrung my hand.

10

It was the custom of the Prefect of Police to send me a report on the condition of the capital and the feeling of the people. Sapt read out his report the next afternoon as I relaxed in the King's bedroom in the Palace:

His Highness the Duke of Strelsau left the city, accompanied by several of his household. His destination is believed to be the Castle of Zenda. De Gautet, Bersonin, and Detchard followed an hour later, the last-named carrying his arm in a sling.

"Then we come to this," said Sapt:

Madame de Mauban left for Dresden by train at midday. The Dresden train stops at Zenda.

The king is much criticised by his people for taking no steps about his marriage. They are coupling Princess Flavia's name with that of the Duke of Strelsau, and the duke gains much popularity from the suggestion. I have made an announcement that the King gives a ball tonight in honour of the princess, and the effect is good.

"That is news to me," I remarked in surprise.

"Oh, the preparations are all made!" laughed Fritz. "I've seen to that. Look here, I hate telling you this, but I've been told that the princess has become most attached to the King since the coronation, and is deeply wounded by the King's neglect."

"Here's a kettle of fish!" I groaned.

"I think," said Sapt, "that you'd better make your offer tonight at the ball."

"Good heavens, no!"

"All right, lad, all right," he said. "We mustn't press you too hard."

The ball was a sumptuous affair. I opened it by dancing with Flavia. Curious eyes and eager whispers attended us. We went in to supper; and half-way through, half mad by then in my love for her, I rose in my place before the brilliant crowd, and taking off the yellow and red ribbon with its jewelled badge that I was wearing, I flung it round her neck. In a tumult of applause I sat down. The rest of the meal passed in silence. Fritz touched me on the shoulder, and I rose, gave Flavia my arm, and walked down the hall into a little room, where coffee was served to us. The gentlemen and ladies in attendance withdrew, and we were alone.

I looked at her and forgot the King in Zenda, I forgot the King in Strelsau. I even forgot that she was a princess — and I an impostor. I threw myself on my knee and pressed my kisses on her lips.

She pushed me from her, crying suddenly:

"Ah! Is it true? Or is it only because you must?"

"It's true!" I said, in low tones, "true that I love you more than life — or truth — or honour!"

"How is it that I love you now, Rudolf?"

"Now?"

"Yes — just lately. I - I never did before."

"Never before?" I asked eagerly.

She laughed.

"You speak as if you would be pleased to hear me say 'Yes' to that," she said.

"Would 'Yes' be true?"

"Yes," I heard her just breathe, and she went on in an instant: "Be careful, Rudolf. He will be mad now."

"Who, Michael? If Michael were the worst —"

"What worse is there?"

There was yet a chance for me. Controlling myself with a mighty effort, I took my hands off her and stood a yard or two away.

"If I were not the King," I began, "if I were only a private gentleman...."

Before I could finish, her hand was in mine.

"If you were a convict in the prison of Strelsau, you would be my King," she said.

Under my breath I groaned, "God forgive me!" and, holding her hand in mine, I said again:

"If I were not the King...."

"Ah, Rudolf! Does a woman who marries without love look on the man as I look on you?"

"Flavia," I said, in a strange dry voice, "I am not...."

A little cry burst from Flavia, as she sprang back from me. My half-finished sentence died on my lips. Sapt stood there, bowing low, but with a stern frown on his face.

"A thousand pardons, sire," said he, "but his Eminence the Cardinal has waited this quarter of an hour to offer his respectful adieu to your Majesty."

I looked at his eyes and read in them an angry warning. How long he had been a listener I knew not, but he had come upon us in the nick of time.

"We must not keep his Eminence waiting," said I.

Flavia held out her hand to Sapt. He looked at her radiant eyes and blushing face. A sad smile passed over the old soldier's face, and there was a tenderness in his voice as, bending to kiss her hand, he said:

"In joy and sorrow, in good times and bad, God save your Royal Highness!"

Then drawing himself up, he added, "But, before all comes the King — God save the King!"

And Flavia caught my hand and kissed it, murmuring, "Amen! Good God, Amen!"

We went into the ballroom again. Forced to receive adieus, I was separated from Flavia. I faced all Strelsau that night as the King and the accepted suitor of the Princess Flavia.

At last, at three in the morning, I was in my dressing room. Only Sapt was with me. As I sat like a man dazed, he puffed at his pipe. On the table by me lay a rose. It had been in Flavia's dress, and, as we parted, she had kissed it and given it to me.

Sapt advanced his hand towards the rose, but, with a quick movement, I put mine down upon it.

"That's mine," I said, "not yours — nor the King's either."

"I know what's on your mind," said Sapt. "But, lad, you're bound in honour."

"You can spare me that, Sapt," I said. "If you would not have your King rot in Zenda, while Michael and I play for the great stake outside, we must act quickly! Let's go to Zenda and crush Michael and bring the King back to his own again."

The old fellow stood up and looked at me for a full minute.

"And the princess?"

I bowed my head to meet my hands, and crushed the rose between my fingers and my lips.

I felt his hand on my shoulder as he whispered low in my ear:

"Before God, you're the finest Elphberg of them all. But I have eaten of the King's bread, and I am the King's servant. Come, we will go to Zenda!"

I looked up and caught his hand. And the eyes of both of us were wet.

11

It was a cold morning when I walked, unattended, to the princess's house, carrying a nosegay in my hand. Every attention I paid her bound me closer to the people, who worshipped her. I found Countess Helga, the princess's companion, gathering flowers. I requested her to take mine in their place. We were talking on the broad terrace that ran along the house. A window above our heads stood open.

"Madame!" cried the countess merrily, as Flavia looked out. I bared my head and bowed.

"Bring him in, Helga," she said, "I'll give him some coffee."

The countess led the way and took me into Flavia's morning room, and then left us. The princess laid two letters before me. One was from Black Michael — a most courteous request that she honour him by spending a day at his Castle of Zenda, as had been her custom every summer. I threw down the letter in disgust, and Flavia laughed at me. Then, growing grave again, she pointed to the other sheet.

"I don't know who wrote it," she said. "Read it."

I knew in a moment. There was no signature at all this time, but the handwriting was the same as that which had told me of the snare in the summerhouse: it was Antoinette de Mauban's. The letter ran thus:

I have no cause to love you, but God forbid that you should fall into the power of the duke. Accept no invitations of his, go nowhere without a large guard. Show this, if you can, to him who reigns in Strelsau.

"Why doesn't it say 'the King'?" asked Flavia. "Is it a hoax?"

"Obey it to the very letter," I said. "A regiment shall camp around your house today. Do not go out unless well guarded."

"You know who sent it?"

"I can guess," said I. "It is from a good friend — and I fear, an unhappy woman. Make your excuses, Flavia, to the duke. Don't go."

I left her and returned to the Palace. I summoned Sapt and Fritz and told them that the King's plans to go on a hunting trip the next day should be made public.

About five miles from Zenda — on the opposite side from that on which the Castle is situated — there lies a large tract of wood. It is rising ground, and on it stands a fine modern chateau, the property of a distant kinsman of Fritz's, the Count Stanislas von Tarlenheim. He seldom visited the house, and had, on Fritz's request, very readily and courteously offered me its hospitality for my party and myself. This, then, was our destination. This chateau was within striking distance of the Duke of Strelsau's more magnificent Castle on the other side of the town. A large party of servants, with horses and luggage, started early in the morning. At midday, we followed them, travelling by train for thirty miles, and then mounting our horses to ride the remaining distance to the chateau.

Besides Sapt and Fritz, ten gentlemen accompanied me. They were told part of the truth: the attempt on my life in the summerhouse by Michael's men was revealed to them. They were also informed that it was suspected that a friend of the King's was being forcibly confined within the Castle of Zenda. His rescue was one of the objects of the expedition. Young, brave, and loyal, they asked no more: they were ready to prove their dutiful obedience, and prayed for a fight as the best mode of showing it.

Thus the scene was shifted from Strelsau to the chateau of Tarlenheim and the Castle of Zenda. My task was to get the King out of the Castle alive. Force was useless. I already had an idea of what we must do. Michael must know by now of my expedition. And I knew him too well to suppose that he would be blinded by the story of the hunt. He would understand very well who the real quarry was. That, however, had to be risked.

Also, I knew Michael would not believe that I meant well by the King. In his own way he loved the princess. Would he kill the King? Ay, verily, that he would. But he would kill Rudolf Rassendyll first, if he could.

Michael certainly knew of my arrival, because within an hour an imposing Embassy arrived from him, including the other three of his famous Six — the three Ruritanian gentlemen — Lauengram, Krafstein, and Rupert Hentzau. Young Rupert made us a neat speech, wherein my devoted subject and loving brother, Michael of Strelsau, prayed me to pardon him for not paying his addresses in person, and, further, for not putting his Castle at my disposal. The reason he claimed for both was that he, and several of his servants, lay sick with scarlet fever.

"I hope all beneath your roof are not sick," I said. "What about my good friends, De Gautet, Bersonin, and Detchard? I heard the last had suffered a hurt."

Lauengram and Krafstein looked glum and uneasy, but young Rupert's smile grew broader.

"He hopes to find a medicine for it, sire," he answered.

And I burst out laughing, for I knew what medicine Detchard longed for — it is called Revenge.

After they had departed, Fritz and I rode off to a certain little inn that I knew of, leaving Sapt in the chateau. I muffled myself up in a big cloak.

When we reached the inn, we ordered dinner and wine. I sat down in a private room. The younger daughter of the inn-keeper, who had served me on my first visit, came in with the wine. She looked at me and asked Fritz, "Is the gentleman in great pain?"

"The gentleman is no worse than when you had seen him last," said I, throwing away my cloak.

She gave a little shriek.

"It was the King, then! I told mother so the moment I saw his picture. I must go and tell her."

"Stop," I said. "We are not here for sport tonight. Go and bring dinner, and not a word of the King being here."

She came back in a few minutes.

"Well, how is Johann?" I asked.

"We hardly see him, sire."

"And why not?"

"He's very busy at the Castle, sire, because he is in charge of the house."

"What! Johann turned housemaid?"

The girl was brimming over with gossip.

"They say there is a lady at the Castle, sire. And Johann has to wait on the gentlemen."

"Surely he can find half an hour to come and see you?"

"It would depend upon the time, sire."

"Tell him to meet you at the second milestone out of Zenda tomorrow evening at ten o'clock. Say you will be there and will walk home with him."

"Do you mean him harm, sire?"

"Not if he will do as I bid him. We shall leave now. No one is to know that the King has been here."

When we were out, Fritz asked, "You want to catch this fellow Johann?"

"Ay, and I think I have baited the hook right."

As the hooves of our horses sounded on the gravel, Sapt rushed out to meet us.

"Thank God, you're safe!" he cried. "Have you seen anything of them?"

"Of whom?" I asked, dismounting.

"Lad," he said to me, "you must not ride about here, unless with half a dozen of us. Do you know among our men a tall young fellow, Bernenstein by name?"

"I do."

"He lies in his room upstairs, with a bullet through his arm. He strolled out alone after dinner. He had walked a mile or two into the wood when he thought he saw three men among the trees. One levelled a gun at him. He began to run back towards the house because he had no weapon. But one of them fired, and he was hit. He reached here with great difficulty before he fainted."

He paused and added, "Lad, the bullet was meant for you."

12

The next morning I was lying on a hammock in the sun when Rupert Hentzau cantered up to where I lay. He requested to talk to me privately in order to deliver a message from the Duke of Strelsau. I made everyone withdraw, and then he said, seating himself by me:

"It is well, Rassendyll, that we are alone."

I rose to a sitting posture.

"If you do not know how to address the King, your master must find another messenger."

"Why keep up the farce?" he asked, dusting his boot with his glove.

"Because it is not finished yet; and meanwhile I choose my own name."

"Oh, so be it! Yet I spoke out of love for you; for indeed you are a man after my own heart."

"What is the message?" I asked.

"The duke offers you safe-conduct across the frontier and a million crowns."

I refused and asked instead, "How is your prisoner?"

"The King...?"

"Your prisoner."

"He is alive, sire."

He rose to his feet; I imitated him. Then came the most audacious thing I have known in my life. My friends were some thirty yards away. Rupert called to a groom to bring his horse, and dismissed the fellow. The horse stood near. I stood still, suspecting nothing. Rupert made as though to mount, then he suddenly turned to me, his left hand resting in his belt, his right hand outstretched:

"Shake hands," he said.

I bowed, my hands behind me. Quicker than thought, his left hand darted out at me, and a small

dagger flashed in the air. He struck me in the shoulder — had I not swerved, it would have struck my heart. With a cry, I staggered back. Rupert leapt on to his horse and was off like an arrow, pursued by cries and revolver shots. I sank into my chair, bleeding profusely. My friends surrounded me, and then I fainted.

I awoke weak and weary, but Fritz bade me cheer up, saying that my wound would heal soon, and that all had gone well, for Johann the keeper, had fallen into the snare we had laid for him, and was in the house.

I ordered him to be brought at once. Sapt conducted him, hands tied behind his back, and set him in a chair by my bedside. And here, in brief, is his story:

"Below the level of the ground in the Castle, approached by a flight of stone steps at the end of the drawbridge, are situated two small rooms, cut out of the rock itself. The outer of the two rooms has no windows, but is lighted with candles; the inner has one square window, which faces the moat. In the outer room there lie always, day or night, three of the Six. The instructions of Duke Michael are, that on any attack being made on the outer room, the three were to defend the door so long as they could without risk to themselves. But, if the door were in danger of being forced, then Rupert or Detchard should leave the others to hold it as long as they could, and himself pass into the inner room, and kill the King. He should then unlock the bars in the square window, tie a weight to the body and dragging it to the window, slip it through the great earthenware pipe that passes from the window into the moat. Silently, without splash or sound, it will fall into the water and thence to the bottom of the moat. The others were to seek the same route to escape, after barring the door. Then they would swim to the other side and ride away on their waiting horses. And, if things went wrong, the duke would join them and seek safety in riding away. That is the plan of the duke for the disposal of the King in case of need. But it is not to be used till the last; for he does not want to kill the King unless he can, before or soon after, kill you also, sir."

Sapt, Fritz and I looked at one another in horror and bewilderment at the cruelty and cunning of the plan.

"Does the King know this?" I asked.

"My brother and I put up the pipe, sir, under the orders of my Lord of Hentzau. The King grew white when he looked on the pipe."

"If anyone asks you if there is a prisoner in Zenda, you may answer 'Yes.' But do not, if you value your life, say who the prisoner is," I warned him.

Johann was led away. When he had gone, I said to Sapt, "It's a hard nut!"

"So hard," said he, "that I think next year you will still be the King of Ruritania!"

"There seem to be two ways by which the King can come out of Zenda alive. One is by treachery in the duke's followers."

"You can leave that out," said Sapt.

"I hope not," I rejoined, "because the other I was about to mention is — by a miracle from heaven!"

13

Sapt and I, after anxious consultations, resolved that we must strike a blow without wasting time, this resolution being clinched by Johann's news that the King grew pale and ill, and that his health was breaking down under his rigorous confinement.

Late next night after dinner, I changed my clothes and went out. Sapt and Fritz were waiting for me with six men and horses. Over his saddle Sapt carried a long coil of rope, and both men were heavily armed. I had with me a short, stout cudgel and a long knife. Making a circuit, we avoided the town, and in an hour found ourselves slowly mounting the hill that led to the Castle of Zenda.

The night was dark and very stormy; the great trees moaned and sighed. When we came to a thick clump, about a quarter of a mile from the Castle, we bade our six friends hide there with the horses. Sapt had a whistle, and they could rejoin us in a few moments if danger came.

We gained the top of the hill without accident, and found ourselves on the edge of the bank of the moat. Sapt silently and diligently, set to fasten the rope to a tree nearby. I stripped off my boots, took a pull at the flask of brandy Fritz carried, loosened the knife in its sheath, and took the cudgel between my teeth. Then I shook hands with my friends, and laid hold of the rope. I was going to have a look at the pipe.

I lowered myself very gently into the water, struck out and began to swim round the great walls. I could see lights from the Castle on the other side, and now and again I heard laughter and merry shouts. I moved very slowly, looking for the pipe. Out of the darkness ahead, it came into view. I was about to approach it, when I saw something else, and my heart stood still. The nose of a boat protruded beyond the pipe on the other side. I listened intently. I heard a slight shuffle — as of a man shifting his position. Who was the man guarding Michael's invention? Was he awake or asleep? I trod water and found the ground under my feet. The foundations of the Castle extended some fifteen inches, making a ledge. I stood on it, out of the water from my armpits upwards.

There was a man in the boat, with a rifle next to him. By his deep breathing, I could tell he was fast asleep. Kneeling on the shelf, I drew forward under the pipe till my face was within two feet of his. It was Johann's brother. I drew out the knife. Of all the deeds of my life, I love the least to think of this. I said to myself, "It is war — and the King's life is at stake." I raised the knife and struck home.

Leaving him where he lay, I leaned over the pipe and examined it, from the end near the water to the topmost extremity, where it passed through the masonry of the wall. Dropping on my knees, I tested the underside. And my breath went quick and fast, for on the lower side, where the pipe should have clung to the masonry, there was a gleam of light! That light must come from the cell of the King! I put my shoulder against the pipe and exerted my strength. The chink widened a very, very little. I now knew that the pipe was not fixed in the masonry at the lower side. Then I heard a voice — a harsh, grating voice. It was Detchard's.

"Have you anything to ask, sire, before we part?"

The King replied in a faint and hollow voice.

"Pray my brother," said the King, "to kill me. I am dying by inches here."

"The duke does not desire your death, sire — yet," sneered Detchard.

"Then leave me alone."

The light disappeared. I heard the door being bolted, and then I heard the sobs of the King.

I dared not do anything more that night. My task now was to get back safely.

I returned to where my friends waited, and hailed Sapt in a low tone. The rope came down. I tied it round the corpse and then went up it myself. Suddenly three men on horseback swept round from the front of the Castle.

"The devil, but it's dark!" cried a ringing voice

A moment later, shots rang out. Our people hiding in the woods had met them. A fierce fight followed.

Holding on to the cudgel, I ran and came face to face with a man on a horse. It was Rupert Hentzau.

"At last!" I cried.

"It's the play-actor!" cried he, slashing my cudgel in two.

I ducked my head and scampered for my life. Rupert, who had my men chasing him, went full gallop to the edge of the moat and leapt in, while the shots of our party fell thick around him. But, in the darkness, he swam to the corner of the Castle, and vanished from our sight.

Our men had killed Lauengram and Krafstein. We flung them into the moat and rode off down the hill and back to our chateau.

One day, soon after the incident at the Castle, I was riding in the town of Zenda, when I met the Head of the Strelsau Police.

"What brings you here?" I asked.

"I am here because a young countryman of the British Ambassador is missing, sire. His friends have not heard from him in two months, and there is reason to believe that he was last seen in Zenda. The officials at the railway recollect his name on some luggage."

"What is his name?"

"Rassendyll, sire," he answered. "It is thought that he may have followed a lady here. Has your Majesty heard of a certain Madame de Mauban?"

"Why, yes," said I, my eyes travelling to the Castle. "Sapt, I must have a word with the Prefect privately. Will you please ride a few paces ahead?"

And then I added to the Prefect: "Come, sir. What is it that you have to say?"

"Nothing has been heard of this Rassendyll for two months." And this time the eyes of the Prefect travelled towards the Castle.

"Yes, the lady is there," I said quietly. "But I don't know where Mr Rassendyll — is that the name? — is."

"The duke," he whispered, "does not like rivals, sire."

"You're right there," said I, with all sincerity. "But surely you hint at a very grave charge?"

He spread his hands out in apology.

I whispered in his ear, "Go back to Strelsau. Tell the Ambassador that you have a clue, but that you must be left alone for a week or two. Meanwhile, I'll look into the matter."

He promised to obey me, and I rode on to rejoin Sapt. I realised that inquiries about me must be stopped at all hazards for a week or two.

We were by now at the extreme end of the town, just where the hills begin to mount towards the Castle. We saw a cortège winding slowly down the hill. There came first two mounted servants in black uniforms, followed by a car drawn by four horses: on it, under a heavy pall, lay a coffin; behind it rode a man in plain black clothes, carrying a hat in his hand.

I beckoned to my groom.

"Ride and ask whom they escort," I ordered.

He rode up to the servants, and I saw a gentleman ride back with him. It was Rupert Hentzau.

"Your Majesty asks whom we escort," said Rupert. "It is my dear friend Albert of Lauengram."

"Sir, no one regrets the unfortunate affair more than I."

"Your Majesty's words are gracious," he said. "I grieve for a friend. Yet, sire, others must soon lie as he lies now."

"It is a thing we all would do well to remember, my lord," I rejoined. "How fares my brother?"

"He is better, sire. He hopes soon to leave for Strelsau."

Rupert signed to his party to proceed. I suddenly decided to ride after him. He turned, fearing an attack.

"You fought as a brave man the other night," I said. "If you deliver your prisoner alive to me, you shall come to no hurt."

Rupert lowered his voice to a whisper. "I have a proposal for you. Attack the Castle boldly. Sapt and Fritz will fall; Black Michael will fall —"

"What!"

"— Black Michael will fall, like the dog he is; the prisoner, as you call him, will go down the pipe — ah, you know that! Two men will be left — Rupert Hentzau and you, the King of Ruritania. Isn't that a hand to play — a throne and your princess?"

"Get out of my reach!" said I.

I rode back to Tarlenheim with Sapt, trying to hide my shock and anger — shock at Rupert's disloyalty, and anger for looking on the princess as a trophy. There, a servant handed me a note. It was unaddressed.

"Is it for me?"

"Yes, sire; a boy brought it."

I tore it open:

Johann carries this for me. I warned you once. In the name of God, and if you are a man, rescue me from this den of murderers! - A de M.

14

After the meeting with Rupert Hentzau, there was a marked effect on the garrison of Zenda. They ceased to be seen abroad; and my men reported that utmost vigilance prevailed there. Michael bade me defiance; and although he had been seen outside the walls, he did not take the trouble to send any excuse for his failure to wait on the King. Time ran on in inactivity, when every moment was pressing; for not only was I faced with the new danger which the stir about my disappearance

brought on me, but greater murmurs had arisen in Strelsau at my continued absence from the city.

As a final blow, nothing would content my advisers, the Chancellor and Marshal Strakencz, save that I should appoint a day for the public solemnisation of my betrothal, a ceremony which in Ruritania is as great and binding a thing as the marriage itself. This I was forced to do, as Flavia was with me at the chateau at the moment. She had rushed here on hearing about my injury, escorted by Marshal Strakencz, and now refused to leave my side. I set a date a fortnight ahead, appointing the Cathedral in Strelsau as the place. And this formal act being published far and wide, caused great joy throughout the kingdom.

I did get some news of the Castle when Johann, greedy for more money, again found an opportunity to visit us. He had been waiting on the duke when the tidings of my betrothal arrived. Black Michael's face had grown blacker still, and he had sworn savagely.

What caused me great worry was Johann's news that the King was very sick: Johann had seen him. He was, he said, wasted and hardly able to move. So alarmed were the men at the Castle that they had sent for a physician from Strelsau. The physician had come forth from the cell pale and trembling, and urgently prayed to the duke to let him return, but the duke refused. Instead, he held him a prisoner, telling him his life was safe if the King lived.

"And how do they guard the King now?" I asked, remembering that two of the Six were dead.

"Detchard and Bersonin watch by night, Hentzau and De Gautet by day, sir," he answered.

"Only two at a time?"

"Ay, sir, but the others rest in a room just above, and are within sound of a cry or a whistle."

"Is there any communication between it and the room they watch?"

"No, sir. You must go down a few stairs and through the door by the drawbridge, and so to where the King is lodged."

"And that door is locked?"

"Only the four lords have the keys, sir."

I drew nearer to him.

"Where does the duke lodge?"

"In the chateau, on the first floor. His apartments are on the right as you go towards the drawbridge."

"And Madame de Mauban?"

"Just opposite, on the left. But her door is locked after she has entered."

"And the duke, I suppose, has the key?"

"Yes, sir. The drawbridge is drawn back at night, and of that, too, the duke holds the key, so that it cannot be run across the moat without application to him."

"Where do you sleep?"

"In the entrance hall of the chateau, with five servants."

"Armed?"

"They have pikes, sir, but no firearms."

Now I took the matter boldly into my hands. I had failed once at the entrance of the pipe; I would fail again if I went that way. I must make the attack from the other side.

"Do these servants know who the prisoner is?"

"No, sir."

"You shall have fifty thousand crowns if you do what I ask you tomorrow night. At two in the morning exactly, fling open the front door of the chateau."

"Will you be there, sir?"

"Ask no questions. Do what I tell you."

"And can I escape by the door, sir, after I have opened it?"

"Yes, as quick as your legs will carry you. Take this note to Madame and tell her, for the sake of all our lives, not to fail in what it orders."

When the fellow was gone, I called Sapt and Fritz and unfolded the plan I had formed. Sapt shook his head.

"Why can't you wait?"

"The King may die."

The plan I had made was like this. A strong party under Sapt's command was to steal up to the door of the chateau. If discovered, they were to kill anyone who found them — with their swords, for I wanted no noise of firing. If all went well, they would be at the door when Johann opened it. They were to rush in and secure the servants. At the same time — and on this hinged the plan — a woman's cry was to ring out loud and shrill from Antoinette de Mauban's chamber. Again and again she was to cry, "Help, help! Michael, help!" And then she was to utter the name of Hentzau. Then, as we hoped, Michael, in fury, would rush out of his apartments opposite, and fall alive into the hands of Sapt. Still the cries would go on; and my men would let down the drawbridge. It would be strange if Rupert, hearing his name, did not descend from where he slept and seek to cross the drawbridge. Perhaps De Gautet would accompany him.

And when Rupert put his foot on the drawbridge? I would be there to challenge him. I planned to swim in the moat as I had earlier. This time, I would carry a small wooden ladder on which I could rest my arms in the water — and my feet, when I left it. I would place it against the wall just by the bridge and stealthily climb up to the drawbridge. However, if I was late and Rupert or De Gautet had already crossed in safety, it would be my misfortune, not my fault. But if I managed to kill them, then only two of the Six would remain.

Perhaps they would rush out. If they stood by their orders, then the King's life hung on the swiftness with which we could force the outer door. Our first priority would be therefore, to secure the keys to the doors of the all-important rooms.

So I planned — desperately. And, that our enemy might be better lulled to security, I gave orders that our residence should be brilliantly lighted from top to bottom all night, as though we were engaged in revelry. Marshal Strakencz would be there, his job being to conceal our departure from Flavia. And if we did not return by morning, he was to march, openly and in force to the Castle, and demand the person of the King. If Black Michael was not there, as I did not think he would be, the Marshal would take Flavia with him, as swiftly as he could, to Strelsau, and there proclaim Black Michael's treachery and the probable death of the King, and rally everyone round the banner of the princess.

It was late when we rose from the conference. I proceeded to the princess's apartments. We talked a while, and when I took my leave, she slipped a ring on my finger. I took off my ring and put it on her finger, saying, "Wear that ring, even though you wear another when you are queen."

"Whatever else I wear, this I will wear till I die and after," said she, and kissed the ring.

15

The night came fine and clear. At twelve o'clock, Sapt's party left the chateau and struck off to the right, avoiding the town of Zenda. If all went well, they would be in front of the castle by about a quarter to two. Leaving their horses half a mile off, they were to steal up to the entrance and hold themselves in readiness for the opening of the door. If the door was not opened, they were to send Fritz round to the other side of the castle. I would meet him there if I was alive, and we would consult whether to storm the Castle or not. If I was not there, they were to return with all speed to the chateau, rouse the Marshal, and march in force to Zenda.

I mounted my horse. I was covered with a large cloak, and under this I wore warm, tight-fitting clothes, and light canvas shoes. I had rubbed myself thoroughly with oil, and carried a large flask of whisky. Also I tied round my body a length of thin but stout cord, and I did not forget my ladder.

I took a shorter route and found myself in the outskirts of the forest at about half-past twelve. I tied up my horse in a clump of trees, leaving the revolver in its pocket in the saddle — it would be of no use to me. Ladder in hand, I made my way to the edge of the moat. Here I unwound my rope, bound it securely round the trunk of a tree on the bank and let myself down. I pushed the ladder before me as I swam, and hugging the Castle wall, I finally came to the pipe. I crouched down in the shadow of the great pipe and waited.

Suddenly the duke's window grew bright. The window was flung open and I saw Antoinette de Mauban look out. A moment later, a man came and tried to put his arm round her waist, but with a swift motion she sprang away. It was young Rupert. He was about to lay his hand on her again, when there was a noise of a door in the room opening, and a harsh voice cried, "What are you doing here, sir?"

Black Michael, for it was he, advanced towards the window. He caught young Rupert by the arm.

"Does your Highness threaten me?" asked Rupert.

"Enough, Rupert, enough! We mustn't quarrel. Are Detchard and Bersonin at their posts?"

"They are, sir."

"Then, sir, please leave us."

Rupert left the room. The duke shut the window and moved away with the lady.

De Gautet and Rupert crossed the drawbridge to the Castle and it was drawn up after them.

Ten minutes later, I heard a slight noise on my right, and, peering over the pipe, I saw a dark figure standing in the gateway that led to the bridge. It was Rupert. To my surprise, he began to climb down the wall. When he came to the lower step, he put his sword between his teeth, turned round, and noiselessly let himself into the water. I watched him with intense eagerness.

He swam quietly across to the chateau. He climbed the steps on the other side, and when he came to the gateway, I heard him unlock the door. I could hear no noise of its closing behind him. He vanished from my sight.

I swam to the side of the bridge and climbed halfway up the steps by the side of the Castle. There I hung with my sword in my hand, listening eagerly. Not a sound broke the silence.

There were plots, I said to myself, other than mine afoot in the Castle that night.

16

As I waited, I thought to myself that I had at least scored one point. Rupert was on the other side of the moat from the King. All was still at the chateau. The window of the duke's room remained shuttered. A light burnt steadily in Madame de Mauban's window. I looked around and saw that the gateway to the drawbridge was broader than the bridge; there was a dark corner on the opposite side where a man could stand without being seen. I darted across and stood there. Then I heard the faintest sound made by a key being turned very carefully and slowly. It came from behind the door which led to the drawbridge on the other side of the moat.

The next moment — before my friends could be near the chateau door — there was a sudden crash from the room with the lighted window. It sounded as though someone had flung down a lamp; and the window went dark. At the same instant a cry rang out, shrill in the night: "Help, help! Michael, help!" This was followed by a shriek of utter terror.

There was another shriek. Then I heard the handle of a door being savagely twisted.

"Open the door! In God's name, what's the matter?" cried a voice — the voice of Black Michael himself.

He was answered by the very words I had written in my letter.

"Help, Michael — Hentzau!"

A fierce oath rang out from the duke, and with a loud thud he threw himself against the door. At the same moment I heard a window above my head open, and a voice cry out, "What's the matter?"

Then I heard a man's hasty footsteps. I grasped my sword. If I could kill De Gautet, the Six would be less by one more.

Next I heard the clash of crossed swords and a tramp of feet. There was an angry cry from Antoinette de Mauban's room, the cry of a wounded man. The window was flung open and then Rupert stood on the window sill, sword in hand. He turned around and said as he slashed out with his sword, "Ah, Johann, there's one for you! Come on, Michael!"

Johann! Had Rupert killed him? Then — how would he open the door for me?

"Help," cried the duke's voice, weak and faint.

I heard a step on the stairs above me, but before anything happened on my side of the moat, I saw five or six men round Rupert. He slashed his sword at them, laughing, as he flung himself headlong into the moat.

As he leapt, De Gautet's face looked out through the door by my side. Without a moment's hesitation, I struck at him with all the strength God had given me, and he fell dead in the doorway without a word or a groan.

I dropped on my knees, looking for the keys, my hands fumbling with excitement. At last I found them. There were but three. Seizing the largest, I felt for the lock that led to the cell. The key fitted and the lock turned. I drew the door close behind me and locked it as noiselessly as I could, putting the key in my pocket.

I found myself at the top of a flight of steep stone stairs. An oil lamp burnt dimly in the bracket. I took it down, stood and listened.

"What the devil can it be?" I heard a voice say.

It came from behind the door that faced me at the bottom of the stairs.

Another answered, "Shall we kill him?"

"Wait a bit," I heard Detchard say. "There'll be trouble if we strike too soon."

There was a moment's silence. Then I heard the bolt of the door being cautiously drawn back. I instantly put out the light I held, replacing the lamp in the bracket.

"It's dark — the lamp is out. Have you a light?" said the other voice — Bersonin's.

I was sure they had a light, so before they could act, I rushed down the steps and flung myself against the door. Bersonin had unbolted the door and it gave way before me. The Belgian stood sword in hand, and Detchard was sitting on a couch at the side of the room. In his astonishment at seeing me, Bersonin recoiled; Detchard jumped to his sword. I rushed madly at the Belgian. He gave way before me. I drove him up against the wall, and in a moment he lay on the floor before me. I turned — Detchard was not there. Faithful to his orders, he had rushed straight to the door of the King's cell, opened it and slammed it behind him.

When I forced the door open, this is what I saw: the King was standing in a corner of the room, his fettered hands moving uselessly up and down, and he was laughing horribly in a half-mad manner. Detchard and the doctor were in the middle of the room. The doctor had flung himself on the murderer. Detchard wrenched himself free, and, as I entered, drove his sword through the hapless man.

Then he turned on me, crying, "At last!"

Our swords clashed. By some blessed chance, neither he nor Bersonin were wearing their revolvers. We began to fight, silently, sternly, and hard. He was the most skilful swordsman I had ever met. But even as he pushed me hard, the King, the half-mad, wasted creature that he had become, leapt high, shrieking, "It's cousin Rudolf! Cousin Rudolf! I'll help you, cousin Rudolf!"

Catching a chair in his hands, he came towards us. Hope came to me.

"Come on!" I cried. "Come on! Drive it against his legs."

Detchard replied with a savage thrust. He all but had me.

"Come on! Come on, man!" I cried. "Come on and share the fun!"

The King laughed gleefully, pushing the chair before him.

With an oath Detchard skipped back, and, before I knew what he was doing, he had turned his sword against the King. He made one fierce cut at the King, and the King, with a piteous cry, dropped where he stood. Then Detchard turned to face me again. But in turning he trod in a pool of blood that flowed from the dead physician. He slipped and fell. Like a dart I was upon him. I caught him by the throat and drove my sword through his neck.

I rushed to where the King lay. Was he dead? I dropped on my knees beside him, and bent down to hear if he breathed. But before I could find out, I heard a loud rattle from outside. I knew the sound: the drawbridge was being pushed out. A moment later, it rang home against the wall on my side of the moat. I would be trapped and the King with me, if he lived!

I took my sword and passed to the outer room. Seizing a revolver lying there, I paused to listen. Suddenly I heard the laughter of Hentzau. The laugh told me that my men had not come, for they should have shot Rupert by now. The clock struck half-past two! My God! The door had not been opened! They had gone to the bank, and not finding me there, had returned to the chateau with news of the King's death — and mine.

For a moment, I sank, unnerved, against the door. Then I started up when I heard Rupert cry, "Michael, come and fight for her!"

If it were a three-cornered fight, I told myself, I might yet play my part. I turned the key in the door and looked out.

17

A strange scene met my eyes. The bridge was in place. At the far end, a group of the duke's servants huddled together, their faces pale, their weapons held in front of them. Rupert stood holding the bridge against them, daring them to come or send Black Michael to him. The servants whispered to one another.

By marvellous chance, I was the master. The servants would oppose me no more than they dared to attack Rupert. I had but to raise my revolver, and Rupert would be a dead man. He did not know that I was there. Strangely, I did nothing. I stood and watched in fascination, waiting for the outcome of the scene.

"Michael, you dog! If you can stand, come on!" cried Rupert.

The answer to his taunts came in the wild cry of a woman, "He's dead! My God, he's dead!"

"Dead!" shouted Rupert. "I struck better than I knew!" and he laughed triumphantly. Then he turned to the servants, shouting, "Down with your weapons! I am your master now!"

They would have obeyed, but as he spoke there arose a distant sound of shouts from the other side of the chateau. My heart leapt. It must be my men, come to seek me. The noise continued, but none seemed to heed it. Their attention was on what was happening before their eyes. The group of servants parted and Antoinette de Mauban staggered on to the bridge. She held a revolver in her shaking hand, and, as she tottered, she fired at Rupert. It missed him and struck the woodwork over my head.

Rupert laughed. She took no notice. Instead, with a wonderful effort, she calmed herself till she stood still. Then very slowly, she began to raise her arm again, taking most careful aim.

I looked at Rupert. He would be mad to risk it. But before she got her aim, he bowed and cried, "I can't kill where I've kissed," and before anyone could stop him, he leapt into the moat. At that very moment I heard a rush of feet, and Sapt's voice cried, "God! It's the duke — dead!"

I knew then, that the King needed me no more, and throwing down my revolver, I vaulted over the parapet with my sword in hand, intent on finishing my quarrel with Rupert. I saw his curly head fifteen yards off in the water of the moat.

He swam swiftly and easily. I was weary. For a time I made no sound, but as we rounded the corner, I cried, "Stop, Rupert, stop!"

He looked over his shoulder, but swam on. I put forth all my remaining strength and pressed on. He found the rope which I had left hanging. With a shout of triumph, he caught hold of it and began to haul himself up. I was soon at the rope, and he, hanging in mid air, saw me, but I could not reach him.

He looked startled when he saw me. I think at first he took me for the King. Then he cried out in an incredulous tone:

"Why it's the play-actor! How come you here, man?" He didn't stop, but climbed on till he gained the bank.

I laid hold of the rope, but I paused. He stood on the bank, sword in hand, and could cut my head open or spit me through the heart as I came up. I let go the rope.

"Never mind," said I; "but as I am here, I think I'll stay."

Rupert smiled down, waved his hand to me, and was gone in an instant. Without thinking of danger, I laid my hand on the rope and was up in a moment. I saw him thirty yards off, running like a deer towards the forest. I rushed after him, calling him to stand. He did not heed my call. Unwounded and vigorous, he gained on me at every step. Forgetting everything in the world except him and my thirst for his blood, I pressed on.

It was three o'clock now, and the day was dawning. I could see Rupert a hundred yards ahead of me. I was forced to pause for breath. A moment later, Rupert turned sharply to the right and was lost from my sight.

I thought all was over, and sank to the ground. But I was up again directly, for a scream rang through the forest — a woman's scream. Putting forth the last of my strength, I ran on to the place where he had turned out of my sight. I saw him again, but alas! I could not touch him. He was in the act of lifting a girl down from her horse; doubtless, it was her scream that I had heard. She was probably on her way to an early market at Zenda. Her horse was a swell, stout, well-shaped animal. Rupert lifted her down amid her shrieks — the sight of him frightened her; but he treated her gently, laughed, kissed her, and gave her money. Then he jumped on the horse and waited for me. I, on my part, waited for him.

Presently he rode towards me, keeping his distance, however. He lifted up his hand, saying, "What did you do in the Castle?"

"I killed three of your friends," said I.

"What! You got to the cells?"

"Yes."

"And the King?"

"He was hurt by Detchard before I killed Detchard, but I pray that he lives."

"You fool!"

"I spared your life. I was behind you on the bridge, with a revolver in my hand."

"No? That means I was between two fires!"

"Get off your horse and fight like a man," said I.

"Before a lady?" said he, pointing to the girl. "Fie, your Majesty!"

Then in my rage, hardly knowing what I did, I rushed at him. For a moment he seemed to waver. Then

he reined his horse in and stood waiting for me. On I went in my folly. I seized the reins and struck him. He parried and thrust at me. I fell back a pace and rushed at him again. This time I reached his face and laid his cheek open. I darted back before he could strike me. He seemed almost amazed at the fierceness of my attack, otherwise I think he would have killed me. I sank on my knee panting, expecting him to ride at me. And so he would have done, and then and there, I doubt not, that either one or both of us would have died. But at that moment there came a shout from behind us, and, looking around, I saw, just at the turn, a man on a horse. He was riding hard, and carried a revolver in his hand. It was Fritz, my faithful friend. Rupert saw him, and knew that the game was up. He checked his rush at me. Instead, he tossed his hair off his forehead and smiled, and said, "*Au revoir,* Rudolf Rassendyll!"

Then, with his cheek streaming blood, but his lips laughing and his body swaying with ease and grace, he bowed to me, and he bowed to the farm-girl, then waved his hand at Fritz, who was just within range and let fly a shot at him. The shot struck his sword, and he dropped it with an oath, wringing his fingers. He clapped his heels hard on the horse's belly, and rode away at a gallop.

Once again he turned to wave his hand, and then vanished through the thickets. I flung my sword down and cried to Fritz to ride after him. But Fritz stopped his horse, leapt down and ran to me. Kneeling, he put his arms about me. The wound that Detchard had given me had broken forth afresh, and my blood was staining the ground.

"Then give me the horse!" I cried, staggering to my feet and throwing his arms off me. The strength of my rage carried me as far as the horse stood, and then I fell beside it.

"My friend — dear friend!" said Fritz, as tender as a woman, kneeling beside me again.

"Is the King alive?"

"Thanks to the most gallant gentleman that lives," said he softly, "the King is alive!"

The farm-girl stood by, weeping and wide-eyed with wonder.

When I heard that the King was alive, I strove to cry "Hurrah!" but could not speak. Instead I laid my head back on Fritz's arm and closed my eyes.

18

The King's rescue being thus successfully concluded, it was now up to Colonel Sapt to ensure that the King's imprisonment was kept a secret. Antoinette de Mauban and Johann were sworn to reveal nothing. The King, wounded almost to death by the jailer who guarded him, had at last recovered, and rested now, wounded but alive, in Black Michael's own room. There he had been carried, his face covered with a cloak, from the cell. Meanwhile messengers were sent at full speed to the chateau, to tell Marshal Strakencz to assure the princess of the King's safety and to come himself with all speed to greet the King.

The princess insisted on accompanying the Marshal.

Meanwhile, I had recovered from my faint, and walking slowly with Fritz's help, I reached the edge of the forest. I saw Flavia riding in her carriage up the hill. I sank on my knees behind a clump of bushes. But there was one whom we had forgotten, the little farm-girl. Hoping to earn maybe a crown or two, she ran to Flavia, curtseying and crying, "Madame, the King is here — in the bushes! May I guide you to him, Madame?"

"Nonsense, child!" said old Strakencz, "the King lies wounded in the Castle."

"Yes, sir, he is wounded, I know, but he is there — with Count Fritz — and not at the Castle."

"Is he in two places, or are there two Kings?" asked Flavia, bewildered. "I will go and see this gentleman," she said, and she rose to alight from the carriage.

But at that moment Sapt came riding from the Castle, and seeing the princess, made the best of a bad job, and cried to her that the King was well tended and in no danger.

"But this girl says that he is yonder — with Count Fritz."

Sapt turned his eyes on the child with a smile and said, "Every fine gentleman is a King to such."

"Why, he's as like the King as one pea to another, Madame!" cried the girl.

Sapt was startled and turned around. "I'll ride myself and see this man," he said hastily.

"Nay, I'll come myself," said the princess.

"Then come alone," he whispered.

Obedient to this strange command, she bade the Marshal and the rest to wait. She and Sapt came on foot towards where we lay, Sapt waving to the farm-girl to keep at a distance. When I saw them coming, I sat in a sad heap on the ground and buried my face in my hands. I could not look at her. Fritz knelt by me, laying his hand on my shoulder.

"Speak low, whatever you say," I heard Sapt whisper to the princess as they came up. The next thing I heard was a low cry — half of joy, half of fear — from the princess.

"It is he! Are you hurt?"

And she fell on the ground by me, and gently pulled my hands away. I kept my eyes to the ground.

"It is the King!" she said. "Pray, Colonel Sapt, tell me, why did you play a joke on me?"

None of us answered. She threw her arms around my neck and kissed me. Then Sapt spoke in a low hoarse whisper:

"It is not the King. Don't kiss him. He's not the King."

She drew back a moment, then with her arms still around my neck, asked, "Do I not know my love, Rudolf?"

"It is not the King," said Sapt again.

A sudden sob broke from the tender-hearted Fritz. It was the sob that told her that what she heard was the truth.

"He is the King!" she cried. "It is the King's face — the King's ring — my ring! It is my love!"

"Your love, Madame," said Sapt, "but not the King. The King is there in the Castle. This gentleman..."

Taking my face between her hands, she cried, "Look at me, Rudolf! Look at me! Why do you let them torment me? Tell me what it means!"

Then I spoke, gazing into her eyes, "God forgive me, Madame!" I said. "I am not the King!"

I felt her hands clutch my cheeks as she gazed at me. And I, silent again, saw wonder born, and doubt grow, and terror spring to life as she looked. And very gradually the grasp of her hands slackened. She turned to Sapt, to Fritz, and back to me, then suddenly reeled forward and fell into my arms. With a cry of pain, I gathered her to me.

Sapt laid his hand on my arm. I looked up at his face. Then I laid her softly on the ground and stood up, looking on her, cursing that young Rupert's sword had spared me for this sharper pang.

19

It was night, and I was in the cell where the King had lain in the Castle of Zenda. The great pipe was gone. All was still. Presently Johann brought me supper. He told me the King was doing well and that he had seen the princess. She and the King, Sapt and Fritz, had been long together.

I sent Johann away. Fritz came into the room. I was standing by the window and idly fingering the cement that clung to the masonry where the pipe had been. He told me that the King wanted to see me. Together we crossed the drawbridge and entered the room that had been Black Michael's.

The King was lying in bed, with the doctor from Tarlenheim in attendance. The King held out his hand and shook mine. Fritz and the doctor withdrew to the window.

I took the King's ring from my finger and placed it on his.

"I have tried not to dishonour it, sire," said I.

"I can't talk much," he said in a weak voice. "I have had a great fight with Sapt and the Marshal. The Marshal now knows everything. I told them that I wanted to take you to Strelsau with me and tell everyone of what you had done. You would have been my best and nearest friend, Cousin Rudolf. But they tell me I must not, and that the secret must be kept."

"They are right, sire. Let me go. My work here is done."

"Yes, it is done, as no man but you could have done it. When my people see me again, I shall have my beard on. Then I shall look like a changed person. Cousin, I shall try to let them find me changed in nothing else. You have shown me how to play the King."

"Sire," said I. "I can take no praise from you. It is by the narrowest grace of God that I was not a worse traitor than your brother."

He turned inquiring eyes on me. His eyes fell on Flavia's ring that I wore. Then he let his head fall on his pillow.

"I don't know when I shall see you again," he said faintly.

"If I can ever serve you again, sire," I answered.

His eyelids closed. I kissed his hand, and let Fritz lead me away. I have never seen the King since.

Outside, Fritz turned and led me, not back towards the drawbridge, but upstairs, through a handsome corridor in the chateau.

Looking away from me, Fritz said, "She has sent for you. When it is over, come back to the bridge. I'll wait for you there."

He opened a door, and gently pushing me in, closed it behind me. At first I thought I was alone, for the light that came from the candles was very dim. But presently I discerned a woman's figure standing by the window. I knew it was the princess, and I walked up to her, fell on my knees, and carried her hand to my lips. She neither spoke nor moved. I rose to my feet, and spoke softly:

"Flavia!"

She trembled a little and looked around. Then she ran towards me and took hold of my hand.

"Don't stand, don't stand! You're hurt! Sit down—here, here!"

She made me sit on a sofa, and put her hand on my forehead.

"How hot your head is!" she said, sinking on her knees by me.

I had come to humble myself and pray for pardon. Instead, I said, "I love you with all my heart and soul! But God forgive me the wrong I have done you!"

"They made you do it!" she said quickly. "It might have made no difference if I had known it. It was always you, never the King!"

"Always?"

"Yes, from the day I saw you."

"I meant to tell you the truth," said I. "I was going to on the night of the ball in Strelsau, when Sapt interrupted me."

"I know, I know! What do we do now, Rudolf?"

"I am going away tonight."

"No! Not tonight!" she cried.

"I must go tonight. Before more people have seen me."

"If I could only come with you," she whispered very low.

"My God!" said I roughly, "don't talk like that!" and I thrust her away from me.

"Why not? I love you. You are as good a gentleman as the King!"

I caught her in my arms then, begging her to come with me and daring all Ruritania to take her from me. For a while she listened, with wondering, dazzled eyes. But as her eyes looked on me, I grew ashamed, and my voice died away and I was silent.

She drew herself away from me.

"Is love the only thing?" she asked in low, sweet tones that seemed to calm my heart. "If love were the only thing, I would follow you to the world's end. But is love everything?"

I made no answer. She came near me and laid her hand on my shoulder.

"If love were the only thing, you would have let the King die in his cell!"

I kissed her hand.

"Honour binds a woman, too, Rudolf. My honour lies in being true to my country and my House. I must stay. Your ring will always be on my finger, your heart in my heart, but you must go and I must stay. Perhaps I must do what it kills me to think of doing."

I knew what she meant. I rose and took her hand.

"Do what you must," said I. "Your ring shall be on my finger and your heart in mine."

I kissed her and then left her.

I walked rapidly down to the bridge. Sapt and Fritz were waiting for me. Under their directions I changed my clothes, and muffling my face, I mounted my horse. We rode through the night and by morning, we reached a roadside station near the border of Ruritania.

When I saw the train coming, I held out my hand to each of them.

Suddenly Fritz uncovered his head and bent as he used to do, and kissed my hand. I snatched it away.

"Heaven doesn't always make the right men kings!" he said.

Old Sapt twisted his mouth as he wrung my hand.

"The devil has a share in most things," said he.

As the train bore me away, I could see that they had bared their heads, and so stood as long as they could see me.

20

When I returned home, my reception was not so alarming as I had feared. It turned out that I had done, not what Rose had wished, but — the next best thing — what she had prophesied. She had declared that I would take no notes, record no observations, gather no materials.

"We've wasted a lot of time trying to find you," she said.

"I know you have," said I. "But why should you have been anxious? I can take care of myself."

"Oh, it wasn't that," she said scornfully, "but I wanted to tell you that Sir Jacob has got an Embassy and wrote to say that he hoped you would go with him."

"Where's he going to?"

"To Strelsau. You couldn't have a nicer place," she said.

"Strelsau!" said I, glancing at my brother. "I don't think I care about it. And I don't think I can go to Strelsau. My dear Rose, would it be — suitable?"

"Oh, nobody remembers that horrid story now."

Upon this, I took out of my pocket a portrait of the King of Ruritania. It had been taken a month or two before he had ascended the throne. She could not miss my point when I said, putting it into her hands:

"In case you have not seen or noticed, look at this picture of Rudolf V. Don't you think they might recall the story, if I appeared in the Court of Ruritania?"

My sister-in-law looked at the portrait and then at me.

"Good gracious!" she exclaimed, and flung the photograph down on the table.

"What do you say, Bob?"

My brother got up, went to a corner of the room, and searched in a heap of newspapers. Presently he came back with a copy of the *Illustrated London News*.

Opening a page, he displayed a double-page picture of the Coronation of Rudolf V at Strelsau. He laid the photograph and the picture side by side. My eyes travelled from my own portrait to Sapt, to the rich robes of the Cardinal, to Black Michael's face, to the stately figure of the princess by his side. I looked long and eagerly. I was roused by my brother's hand on my shoulder. He was gazing at me with a puzzled expression.

"It's a remarkable likeness, you see," said I. "I really think I had better not go to Ruritania."

"That picture in the paper —," my brother began.

"Well, what of it? It shows that the King of Ruritania and I are as alike as two peas."

My brother shook his head.

"I should know you from the man in the picture," he said. "But I must say I am puzzled at the likeness."

"I don't think it's so much like me," I said boldly. "But anyhow, Bob, I won't go to Strelsau."

"No, I don't think it would be wise of you to go to Strelsau, Rudolf," he said.

Since these events, I have lived a very quiet life at a small house I have taken in the country. One break comes every year in my quiet life. Then I go to Dresden, to meet my dear friend and companion, Fritz. For a week Fritz and I are together, and I hear all the news of Strelsau, of the King, and of Flavia. Every year Fritz carries with him to Dresden a little box; in it lies a red rose, and round the stalk is a slip of paper with the words written: 'Rudolf — Flavia — always.' And I also send back a red rose with a similar message. That, and the wearing of the rings are all that now bind us — the Queen of Ruritania and I.

Questions

1

1. Who is the storyteller of the book, *The Prisoner of Zenda*?
2. Why was his sister-in-law annoyed with him?
3. What job would Sir Jacob offer him? When?
4. What did the storyteller plan to do during the next six months?
5. Write about his education. What else did he learn to do?

2

1. Name the places Rudolf visited on his way to Ruritania. Who travelled in the same train?
2. What made Rudolf change his plans? Where did he decide to stay?

3. What did Rudolf learn about the King and his brother at the inn? Was there much love between the brothers?

4. Who was the duke's keeper? Why was he surprised when he saw Rudolf?

5. What did the girl in the inn reply, when Rudolf said, "What does colour matter in a man?"

3

1. Why did Rudolf not take the train directly from Zenda to Strelsau? Write in detail.

2. Describe the castle and its surroundings. What effect did the forest have on Rudolf?

3. Whom did Rudolf see when he opened his eyes? What were they saying to each other?

4. What was the King's reaction when he saw Rudolf? Why was Rudolf surprised to see him? What did the King say, when he heard that Rudolf was going to Strelsau?

5. Where did the King take Rudolf? Who were at the lodge? What did the servant serve the King after he declared that he had drunk enough? Who was it from? What did the King do with it?

4

1. Why did Rudolf awake with a start the next morning? Why were Sapt and Fritz trying to rouse him? Where was the King?
2. Why did Sapt say, "As a man grows old, he believes in Fate"? What did he plan to do?
3. How did Sapt intend to fool the guards who would accompany the King to Strelsau? Where did they keep the King? Whom did they find listening to their conversation? What did Sapt do then?
4. Describe how Rudolf dressed.
5. What did Fritz tell the astonished station master? How long did the train take to reach Strelsau? What happened when the train reached Strelsau?

5

1. Describe briefly what happened after Rudolf stepped out on the platform till he came to the Cathedral.
2. What did Rudolf see when he reached the Cathedral? Describe the coronation ceremony.
3. After he was crowned King, who was the first to wish Rudolf? Who came next?
4. Did anyone look on Rudolf with doubt? Who was in the carriage when he drove to the Palace? What did they discuss?

5. What happened when they reached the Palace?

6

1. Why did Fritz say, "Rassendyll, you mustn't throw your heart too much into the part"?
2. What news did Sapt give Rudolf before they left the Palace? Why was Fritz to let no one into the King's bedroom till the next morning?
3. How did Rudolf and Sapt secretly come out of the palace? Write in detail how Sapt got the city gates opened.
4. Why did Sapt abruptly stop his horse? What did they do when they came to a wood? What did they see and hear?
5. Describe in detail their arrival at the lodge. What did they find in the wine cellar?

7

1. What did Sapt mean when he said, "The King shall be in his capital tomorrow"?
2. When Rudolf warned that the duke knew where the real King was, what was Sapt's reply?
3. Why was it absolutely necessary to have a King in Strelsau?

4. Write in detail why Rudolf was unable to give Josef a decent burial.
5. What did Fritz do when he saw Sapt come in with Rudolf? Who came to visit the King and why?

8

1. Describe Rudolf's first day as King of Ruritania.
2. Who were the Six? Why was Sapt happy to hear that only half of them were in Strelsau?
3. Describe Rudolf's visit to the residence of Princess Flavia.
4. Who visited Rudolf whilst he was there? Describe and name the three gentlemen who were presented to him.
5. What did Princess Flavia mean when she told Rudolf to be careful?

9

1. What was written in the letter Sapt gave Rudolf? Who was it from?
2. Who accompanied Rudolf to the house mentioned in the letter? Describe what he saw there.
3. What did Antoinette de Mauban tell Rudolf? Why was she trying to save Rudolf's life? Did she tell Rudolf where the King was being kept in the castle?

4. Who came to the summerhouse while they were speaking? What offer did they make to Rudolf?
5. How did Rudolf attack them and escape? Write in detail.

10

1. What did the Prefect of the Police send to the King every evening?
2. Write in short the report Sapt read out.
3. Describe the ball in the Palace.
4. What did Rudolf and Flavia discuss after they were served coffee?
5. What happened when Rudolf and Sapt were in the King's dressing room?

11

1. Where did Rudolf go the next morning? What did he carry with him?
2. Who had written the letters to the princess? What did they say?
3. Where did Rudolf and his party go after he left Princess Flavia? Describe the place they went to.
4. What did Rudolf plan to do? What did he think Michael would do?

5. Name the men who came to pay their respects to Rudolf. What excuse did the duke send for not coming himself?

12

1. What offer did Rupert Hentzau bring from the duke?
2. Describe what happened when Rupert asked Rudolf to shake hands.
3. What did Johann tell Rudolf about Michael's arrangements for guarding the King?
4. What warning did Rudolf give Johann?
5. What were the two ways, according to Rudolf, by which the King could come out of Zenda alive?

13

1. What was the news that made Rudolf and Sapt want to strike at the Castle without wasting time?
2. Who went out the next night? Where did they go? What did they carry?
3. What did Sapt do when he came to the bank of the moat? What did Rudolf do? Write in detail.
4. What did Rudolf hear through the pipe?

5. Describe Rudolf's meeting with Rupert Hentzau: (i) near the moat (ii) when Rupert was accompanying the coffin.

14

1. What did Rudolf mean when he said, "As a final blow...."
2. What news did Johann bring that alarmed Rudolf?
3. Write in detail how the King was being guarded. Where were the duke and Madame de Mauban lodged? Where did Johann sleep?
4. What did Rudolf offer Johann if he carried out his orders?
5. What was Rudolf's plan?

15

1. What was Sapt's party instructed to do?
2. How did Rudolf prepare himself for the King's rescue?
3. What did he do when he reached the outskirts of the forest?
4. Where did Rudolf see Madame de Mauban? Describe what followed.
5. Where did Rudolf see Rupert? What did Rupert do?

16

1. What happened while Rudolf stood waiting at the gateway?
2. Describe the fight between Rupert and the duke.
3. What did Rudolf do when De Gautet's face looked out through the door?
4. Narrate what happened when Rudolf burst into the outer room.
5. Describe the scene Rudolf witnessed when he entered the King's cell. How did Rudolf kill Detchard?

17

1. What did Rudolf mean when he said, "By marvellous chance, I was the master"?
2. What did Madame de Mauban cry out when Rupert Hentzau called to Michael to come out and fight? What did she do when she came to the drawbridge? What was Rupert's reaction?
3. What did Rupert say when he heard that the duke was dead? How did he escape?
4. Write in detail what happened after both Rupert and Rudolf had climbed out of the moat.
5. Who came after Rupert had vanished through the thickets? What news did he give Rudolf?

18

1. How was the King carried to the duke's room? Where were messengers sent at once? What message did they carry?
2. What happened when the little girl told the princess that the King was behind the bushes?
3. What did Sapt tell the princess she must do, before he let her go to see for herself?
4. Describe briefly the meeting between Rudolf and the princess.
5. What was the reaction of the princess when Rudolf said, "God forgive me, Madame! I am not the King"?

19

1. Where was Rudolf kept in the Castle? What news did Johann bring?
2. Describe briefly what Rudolf saw when he came into the duke's room, and the conversation he had with the King.
3. Where did Fritz take Rudolf after he left the King? Write briefly what took place.
4. What did the princess mean when she told Rudolf that love was not the only thing?
5. Where did Rudolf go after bidding her farewell?

20

1. What kind of reception did Rudolf receive when he returned home?

2. What did his sister-in-law tell him about Sir Jacob?

3. Why did Rudolf refuse to go to Strelsau? What did Rose think was his reason for not going?

4. Why was Rudolf's brother puzzled when he took out a portrait of the King of Ruritania? What advice did Robert give him?

5. Where did Rudolf settle down? Why did he go to Dresden every year?

List of Headwords

aback	afterwards	angrily
able	again	angry
about	against	animal
above	agitated	announced
abroad	Ah	annoyed
abruptly	ahead	anointed
absence	aim	another
accept	air	answer
accepted	alarmed	answered
accident	alarming	ante-room
accompanied	alas	anxious
accompany	alight	any
accompanying	alike	anyhow
according	alive	anyone
accordingly	all	anything
accustomed	all's	apartments
acknowledge	almost	apology
acquaintance	alone	appeared
across	along	appears
act	aloud	application
action	already	appoint
added	also	appointing
adding	altar	approach
address	although	approached
addressing	always	Archbishop
adieu	am	are
adieus	amazed	arm
advanced	ambassador	armchair
adventures	ambitious	armed
advice	amen	armpits
advisers	amid	arms
affair	among	army
affected	amusement	around
afoot	ancestors	arrangement
afraid	ancestry	arrayed
after	anger	arrival

arrived	bad	begin
arrow	bade	begins
articles	badge	begun
artillery	baited	behind
as	balconies	behold
as though	bald	being
as well as	ball	Belgian
ashamed	ballroom	believe
ask	band	believed
asked	bank	believes
asleep	banner	bells
assume	Bar	belly
assure	bare	belong
astonished	bared	belonged
astonishment	barring	below
at	barrister	belt
at once	bars	bending
ate	battered	beneath
attached	battling	bent
attack	be	berth
attempt	bear	beside
attendance	beard	besides
attendant	bearded	best
attended	bears	bet
attention	beat	betrayed
attracted	beautiful	betrays
au revoir	beauty	betrothal
audacious	because	better
audible	beckoned	between
avenue	become	bewildered
averse	becoming	bewilderment
avoided	bed	beyond
await	bedecked	bid
awaiting	bedroom	big
aware	bedside	bind
away	been	binding
awoke	before	binds
Ay	began	bird
back	begged	bit

122

black	bread	burly
blacker	break	burning
bleeding	breakfast	burnt
blessed	breakfasting	burst
blessings	breaking	bushes
blood	breast	bustle
blow	breath	busy
blowing	breathe	but
blows	breathed	by
blue	breathing	call
blushing	brethren	called
boat	bridge	calling
body	brief	calm
boldly	bright	calmed
bolt	brightly	came
bolted	brilliant	camp
book	brilliantly	can
booking	brimming	candle
boot	bring	candlelight
boots	brings	candles
border	British	candle's
bore	broad	candlestick
born	broader	cannot
both	broke	cantered
bottle	broken	canvas
bottom	brother	cap
bought	brother-in-law	capital
boulevard	brother's	captain
bound	brought	car
bow	brown	Cardinal
bowed	bucket	care
bowing	buffet	career
box	building	careful
boy	buildings	carefully
bracket	bull	cares
brandy	bullet	carriage
brave	burgh	carried
braving	burial	carries
bravo	buried	carry

carrying
cartridge
case
Castle
castles
catch
catching
Cathedral
caught
cause
caused
causing
cautioned
cautiously
ceased
celebrity
cell
cellar
cellars
cells
cement
ceremony
certain
certainly
chair
challenge
chamber
chance
Chancellor
change
changed
chap
charge
charged
charming
chasing
chateau
chatted
checked

cheek
cheeks
cheer
cheering
cheers
child
chink
choked
choose
Christian
chuckled
chuckles
cigar
cigarette
circuit
circumstance
city
claimed
clapped
clapping
clash
clashed
clasping
class
clatter
clattered
clean
clear
clearly
climb
climbed
clinched
clipped
cloak
cloaks
clock
close
closed
closer

closing
clothes
clue
clump
clung
coal-cellar
cocked
coffee
coffin
coil
cold
coldly
collecting
colonel
colour
come
comes
comfort
comfortable
coming
command
commission
communication
community
companion
company
compartment
complete
complexion.
compliment
conceal
concern
concerning
concluded
condition
conduct
conducted
conference
confess

confined	courage	customer
confinement	course	cut
confusion	courteous	dagger
connected	courteously	dancing
conscious	courtesy	danger
consider	cousin	dangerous
considerable	cover	dared
consolation	covered	dared to
consult	crash	daring
consultations	crave	dark
contemplation	creature	darkness
content	credentials	dart
continued	cried	darted
contributing	cries	date
controlling	crimson	daughter
conversation	critical	daughters
convict	crooked	dawning
cool	cross	day
copy	crossed	days
cord	crouched	dazed
cork	crowd	dazzled
corner	crown	dead
corners	crowned	deal
coronation	crowns	dealing
corpse	cruelty	dear
correction	crush	dearest
corridor	crushed	dearly
cortege	cry	death
costumes	crying	debt
couch	cudgel	decent
could	cunning	decided
could not	curious	decidedly
couldn't	curiosity	decision
countess	curly	declared
country	curse	declaring
countryman	cursing	deeds
counts	curtseying	deep
couple	curtsied	deeply
coupling	custom	deer

defiance	dine	doorway
delay	dinner	double
delicately	direct	doubt
delightedly	direction	doubtless
delightful	directly	down
deliver	disappearance	dozen
demand	disappeared	dragging
denounce	discerned	drained
denouncing	discovered	drank
dense	discuss	draught
departed	disfavour	drawbridge
departure	disgust	drawing
depend	dishes	draws
descend	dishonour	drawn
description	disloyalty	dreams
desirable	dismissed	dress
desire	dismounted	dressed
desires	dismounting	dressing
desperately	displayed	drew
destination	disposal	dried
details	disposition	dripping
detected	disquieting	drive
detection	disrespectful	driving
devil	distance	drop
devoted	distant	dropped
dictate	distantly	drove
did	distinguished	drugged
didn't	divide	drunk
die	do	drunken
died	do not	dry
difference	doctor	ducked
different	does	duke
difficulties	doesn't	duke's
difficulty	dog	dusting
dignitaries	doing	duties
dignity	done	dutiful
diligently	don't	dwells
dim	door	dying
dimly	doors	each

eager	enough	expecting
eagerly	ensure	expedition
eagerness	entered	experience
ear	enters	explained
early	entertain	explore
earn	entirely	express
earnestly	entrance	expressed
ears	entry	expression
earthenware	enviable	extended
ease	equal	extreme
easily	erected	extremity
eaten	escape	eye
edge	escort	eyelids
educated	escorted	eyes
effect	especially	face
effort	estates	faced
eh	eternity	faces
eight	Europe	fact
either	even	fail
elder	evening	failing
elderly	events	failure
eleven	ever	faint
else	every	fainted
embarrassed	everybody	faintest
embassy	everyone	faintly
embraced	everything	fair
emerging	exactly	faithful
eminence	examined	fall
empty	excellent	fallen
enchanted	except	family
encloses	excitement	famous
end	exclaim	far
ended	exclaimed	farce
enemy	excursion	fares
engaged	excuse	farewell
English	exerted	farm-girl
Englishman	exorbitant	fascination
enjoy	expect	fashion
enjoying	expected	fashionably

fast	fine	follow
fasten	finely-made	followed
fastened	finest	followers
fat	finger	following
Fate	fingering	folly
father	fingers	fool
father's	finish	foot
fault	finished	footsteps
faults	finishing	for
fear	fire	forbid
feared	firearms	force
fearful	fired	forced
fearing	fires	forcibly
fearless	firing	forehead
feel	firmly	forest
feeling	first	forged
feet	fish	forget
fell	fitted	forgetting
felled	five	forgive
fellow	fixed	forgiveness
felt	flagon	forgot
festivities	flags	forgotten
fetch	flashed	formal
fettered	flask	formed
fever	flat	forming
few	flew	forth
fie	flight	fortnight
fierce	flinch	fortress
fierceness	fling	fortune
fifteen	flinging	forward
fifty	flitted	fought
fight	floor	found
fighter	flowed	foundations
figure	flowers	four
filled	flown	fourteen
final	flung	fraternal
find	flushed	free
finding	fly	French
finds	folded	friend

friends	gazing	gradually
fright	general	grand
frightened	generations	grasp
fro	gentleman	grasped
from	gentlemen	grating
front	gently	grave
frontier	German	gravel
frown	get	great
frowned	getting	greater
frowning	girl	greedy
fulfilling	girls	greet
full	give	greeted
fully	given	greeting
fumbled	giving	grew
fumbling	glad	grey
fun	gladly	grievance
funny	glance	grieve
furnished	glanced	grimly
further	glancing	grimy
fury	glass	grin
future	gleam	groan
gained	gleefully	groaned
gaining	gloomy	groom
gains	glorious	ground
gallant	glove	group
gallop	glum	grow
galloped	go	growing
game	God	growled
garden	goes	grown
garrison	going	grows
gash	gone	guard
gate	good	guarded
gateway	goodnight	guarding
gather	gossip	guess
gathered	got	guide
gathering	grace	gun
gave	graceful	guns
gaze	gracious	ha
gazed	graciously	habits

had	hasty	hero
had always	hat	herself
had been	hate	he's
had failed	hated	hesitate
had suffered	haul	hesitated
had taken	haunt	hesitation
hailed	have	hide
hair	have to	high
half	he	highly
half-mad	head	highness
half-past	headlong	hill
hall	heads	hills
Hallo	heal	him
hammock	health	himself
hand	heap	hinged
handed	hear	his
handkerchief	heard	hissed
handkerchiefs	hearing	historical
handle	heart	hit
hands	hearted	hoarse
handsome	heartily	hoarsely
handwriting	heaven	hoax
handy	heavens	hold
hang	heavily	holding
hanged	heavy	holds
hapless	heed	hollow
happen	heels	holy
happened	height	home
happening	held	honoured
happy	hell	honour
hard	he'll	hoof-beats
harder	helmet	hooves
hardly	help	hook
hare	henchmen	hope
hark	her	hoped
harm	herald	hopefulness
harsh	heralds	hopeless
has	here	hopes
hastily	here's	hoping

horribly	ill	inquiring
horrid	I'll	insisted
horror	illusion	instant
horse	illustrated	instantly
horseback	I'm	instead
horses	imaginary	instructed
horse's	imitated	instructions
hospitality	implements	intelligence
hostess	importance	intend
hot	important	intended
hotel	imposing	intense
hotels	impossible	intent
hound	imposter	intention
hour	in	intently
hours	in a moment	interest
hour's	in fact	interested
house	in front	interesting
household	in silence	interrupted
housemaid	in the hands	into
how	inactivity	introduced
however	incessantly	introduction
huddled	inch	introductions
hugging	inches	invention
humble	incident	invitation
hundred	including	invitations
hundreds	income	invited
hung	inconvenience	invites
hunting	incredulous	iron
hunting-lodge	indeed	is
hurrah	indirect	isn't
hurried	informed	it
hurt	injured	Italian
hush	injury	its
I	inn	it's
I'd	inner	itself
ideal	inn-keeper	I've
idly	inquire	jailer
if	inquiries	jealous

jewelled	knew	leapt
job	knife	learn
join	knighted	least
joined	knock	leave
joke	know	leaving
jot	knowing	led
journey	knowledge	ledge
Jove	known	left
jovial	knows	legs
joy	lad	length
joyful	ladder	lent
jumped	ladies	less
just	lady	let
justice	lady's	letter
keep	laid	letters
keeper	lain	level
keeping	lamp	levelled
kept	land	lie
kettle	language	lies
key	lantern	life
keys	large	lift
kicked	largest	lifted
kidnapped	last	lifter
kill	latch	lifting
killed	late	light
kindly	later	lighted
king	laugh	lightly
kingdom	laughed	lights
kings	laughing	like
king's	laughter	likeness
kinsman	laurels	line
kiss	law	lined
kissed	lay	lips
kisses	lead	listen
knee	leading	listened
kneeling	lean	listener
knees	leaned	listening
knelt	leant	lit

little	mad	meant
lived	Madame	meantime
livery	made	meanwhile
lives	madly	medicine
lock	magnificence	meet
locked	magnificent	men
lodge	Majesty	mention
lodged	make	mere
lodging	making	merriest
lodgings	man	merrily
long	managed	merriment
longed	manner	merry
longer	man's	message
look	many	messenger
looked	marble	messengers
looking	march	met
loosened	mark	midday
lord	marked	middle
lords	market	midst
lose	marriage	might
losing	marries	might be
lost	marry	mighty
lot	marrying	mile
loud	Marshal	miles
love	marvellous	milestone
lovely	masonry	military
loves	mass	million
loving	master	mind
low	material	mine
lower	materials	minute
lowered	matter	minutes
loyal	matters	miracle
loyalest	may	misfortune
luggage	maybe	miss
lulled	me	missed
lump	meal	missing
luncheon	mean	mist
lying	means	moaned

moat	my	nobody
mode	myself	nodded
modern	name	noise
moment	named	noiselessly
moments	names	none
money	narrate	nonsense
month	narrator	nor
months	narrow	nose
moon	narrowest	nosegay
more	nation's	note
morning	nay	notes
most	near	nothing
mother	nearby	notice
mother's	nearer	noticed
motion	nearest	novelist
motionless	neat	now
mount	neck	nowadays
mounted	need	nowhere
mounting	needed	number
mounts	neglect	nut
moustache	neglects	nymph
mouth	neighbourhood	oak
move	neighed	oath
moved	neither	obedience
movement	nerve	obedient
moving	never	obey
much	new	obeyed
muffled	news	objects
murdered	newspaper	observation
murderer	newspapers	observations
murders	next	observe
murmur	nicer	observed
murmured	nick	obtaining
murmuring	night	occasion
murmurs	night's	occupy
must	nine	occurred
mustn't	no	o'clock
muttered	no one	of

off	out	passing
offer	outcome	past
offered	outer	patched
offering	outside	pause
offers	outskirts	paused
office	outstretched	pay
officials	outward	peal
often	outwit	pealed
Oh	over	pealing
oil	overcome	peas
old	overflowing	peered
once	own	peering
one	pace	pen
one by one	paces	people
ones	packed	perfect
only	page	perfectly
open	paid	perhaps
opened	pain	periodicals
opening	pair	permit
openly	palace	person
opens	pale	personages
opportunities	pang	photograph
opportunity	panting	physician
oppose	paper	picked
opposite	parapet	picked up
or	pardon	picture
order	pardons	pictures
ordered	parents	pikes
orderly	park	pillow
orders	parried	pipe
organ	part	piteous
original	parted	place
other	party	placed
others	partying	places
otherwise	pass	plain
ought	passage	plan
our	passed	planned
ourselves	passes	plans

platform	power	proclaimed
play	practice	produced
play-actor	praise	profusely
played	pray	promise
playing	prayed	promised
pleasant	precautions	prompted
please	preceded	property
pleased	Prefect	prophesied
pleasing	preparations	proposal
pleasure	prepared	propped
pledge	preparing	protruded
plentiful	presence	protruding
plots	present	proud
pocket	presented	prove
poetry	presently	public
point	press	published
pointed	pressed	puffed
pointing	pressing	puffing
points	pretended	pull
police	pretty	pulled
politely	prevailed	pursued
politeness	prevent	pursuit
political	price	pushed
Pooh	prince	pushing
pool	princess	put
poor	princess's	putting
Pope	priority	puzzled
popularity	prison	quarrel
portion	prisoner	quarrelling
portly	prisoners	quarter
portrait	private	queen
position	privately	queer
possesses	probable	question
possession	probably	questioning
possible	problems	questioningly
posts	proceeded	questions
posture	procession	quick
pounds	proclaim	quickened

quicker	reception	request
quickly	reckon	requested
quiet	recognises	rescue
quietly	recoiled	residence
quite	recollect	resolution
radiant	record	resolved
rage	recovered	respect
railway	red	respectful
rained	reeled	respectfully
raise	refused	rest
raised	regardless	rested
raising	regiment	resting
rally	regret	retreated
ramble	regrets	return
ran	reigns	returned
rang	rein	returning
range	rejoin	revealed
rapid	rejoined	revelry
rapidly	related	revenge
rapturous	relation	revolver
rather	relatives	revolvers
rattle	relaxed	ribbon
razors	relying	rich
reach	remain	rid
reached	remained	ride
reaction	remaining	rides
read	remark	riding
readily	remarkable	rifle
readiness	remarked	right
ready	remember	rigorous
real	remembering	ring
reality	rent	ringing
realised	repeated	rings
really	replacing	ripe
reason	replied	risen
recall	report	rising
receive	reported	risk
received	repute	rivals

road	sake	seized
roadside	same	seizing
roared	sank	seldom
robes	sat	send
rock	satisfy	sends
rode	savage	sent
rogues	savagely	sentence
rolled	save	separated
romances	saw	series
romantic	say	seriously
roof	saying	servant
room	scampered	servants
rooms	scandal	serve
rope	scarlet	served
rose	scene	service
rot	scholarship	set
roughly	scornfully	set down
round	scraped	setting
rounded	scream	settled
rouse	searched	seven
roving	seasoned	several
royal	seating	shade
rubbed	seats	shadow
ruffians	secluded	shake
ruin	second	shaking
ruling	secret	shall
run	secretly	shan't
running	secure	shaped
rush	securely	share
rushed	security	sharper
ruthless	see	sharply
sacrament	seeing	shave
sad	seek	shaved
saddle	seem	she
safe	seemed	sheath
safely	seems	she'd
safety	seen	sheet
said	sees	shelf

she's	sigh	sleeping
shield	sighed	slender
shifting	sight	slept
shock	sign	slight
shoes	signature	sling
shone	signed	slip
shook	silence	slipped
shooting	silent	slowly
short	silently	small
shorter	silk	smattering
shot	sill	smile
shots	silver	smiled
should	similar	smoked
should not	simply	smote
shoulder	simultaneous	snare
shoulders	since	snatched
shouldn't	sincerity	sneered
shout	singe	so
shouted	single	soap
shouting	sinking	sobs
shouts	sir	social
show	sire	sofa
showed	sirs	softly
showers	sister	soldier
showing	sister-in-law	soldiers
shown	sit	soldier's
shows	sits	solemnisation
shriek	sitting	some
shrieked	situated	someone
shrieks	six	something
shrill	skilful	sometimes
shrubbery	skipped	son
shrugged	slain	soon
shuffle	slammed	sorrow
shut	slapped	sorry
shuttered	slashed	sort
sick	slashing	sought
side	sleep	soul

sound	stamped	stoutly
sounded	stand	straight
Spanish	standing	strange
spare	stands	strangely
spared	staring	stranger
sparing	start	streaming
speak	started	street
speaking	startled	streets
special	stately	strength
speech	station	stretched
speed	stationmaster	stretching
spend	statue	strike
spending	stay	striking
spent	stayed	stripped
spires	steadily	strolled
spirit	steal	strong
spirits	stealthily	stronger
spit	steep	strove
splash	step	struck
splendid	stepped	struck off
split	steps	struggling
spoil	stern	study
spoke	sternly	stunned
spoken	still	stupid
sprang	stilled	subject
spread	stir	subjects
spring	stirred	success
spurred	stole	successfully
spurs	stone	such
square	stood	sudden
staggered	stop	suddenly
staggering	stopped	suffer
stain	stops	sufficient
staining	storey	suggested
staircase	storm	suggestion
stairs	stormy	suitable
stake	story	suitor
stammered	stout	sum

summer	taken	these
summit	taking	they
summoned	talk	they'll
sumptuous	talked	they're
sun	talking	they've
supper	talks	thick
suppose	tall	thickets
sure	task	thigh
surely	tasted	thin
surmounted	taught	thing
surprise	taunts	things
surprising	teeth	think
surrounded	telegraph	thinking
surveyed	tell	thirst
suspected	telling	thirty
suspecting	tells	this
suspicion	temper	thoroughly
swallowed	ten	those
swam	tended	though
swaying	tender	thought
swear	terrace	thousand
swearing	terror	threaten
sweet	tested	threatening
swell	than	three
swept	thank	three-cornered
swerved	thanked	threw
swift	thanks	thrilling
swiftly	that	throat
swiftness	that's	throne
swim	the	throng
sword	their	thronged
swords	them	through
swordsman	themselves	throughout
swore	then	throw
sworn	thence	throwing
swung	there	thrown
table	therefore	thrust
take	there's	thud

thunder	to shoot	train
thus	to sleep	traitor
ticked	to stop	tramp
tidings	to swim	transformed
tie	to take	trap
tied	to talk	trapped
tight-fitting	to think	travel
till	today	travelled
time	together	travelling
times	told	treachery
tiptoe	tomorrow	treated
tired	tone	tree
to	tones	trees
to add	tonight	trembled
to answer	too	trembling
to be	took	trick
to carry	took off	tried
to climb	took out	trip
to defend	took up	tripped
to do	top	triumph
to drink	topic	triumphantly
to face	topmost	trod
to fight	tore	trophy
to get	torment	trot
to hear	torn	trouble
to keep	tossed	truce
to know	tossing	true
to leave	tottered	trumpets
to let	touch	trunk
to make	touched	trust
to play	touches	truth
to prevent	tough	try
to proceed	towards	trying
to read	towered	Tuesday
to reveal	towers	tumbling
to run	town	tumult
to see	tract	turn
to seek	tradition	turned

turning	upwards	wandering
twelve	urged	want
twenty	urgently	wanted
twice	us	wants
twinkled	use	war
twisted	used	warm
twitch	uselessly	warned
two	uselessness	warning
unaddressed	utmost	warrant
unattended	utter	was
unbolted	uttered	wasn't
uncle	valley	waste
uncommonly	vanished	wasted
uncovered	various	watch
under	vaulted	watched
underside	ventured	watching
understand	verily	water
understanding	very	wave
undisturbed	veteran	waved
uneasy	view	waver
unfolded	vigilance	waving
unfortunate	vigorous	way
unhappy	visit	ways
uniform	visited	we
uniforms	visiting	weak
university	visitors	weapon
unless	voice	weapons
unlock	voraciously	wear
unlocked	wagered	wearing
unnamed	waist	weary
unnerved	wait	Wednesday
unused	waited	week
unwound	waiting	weeks
unwounded	walk	weight
up	walked	well
upon	walking	we'll
upset	wall	well-shaped
upstairs	walls	went

were	will not	worse
we're	winding	worshipped
wet	window	worst
we've	windows	worth
what	wine	would
whatever	wine-cellar	would be
what's	wines	would not
when	wisdom	wouldn't
where	wise	wound
wherein	wished	wounded
where's	wishing	wrap
whether	with	wrath
which	withdraw	wrench
while	withdrew	wrenched
whilst	within	wringing
whisky	without	wrinkled
whisper	witnessed	write
whispered	woke	writing
whispering	woman	written
whistle	women	wrong
white	won	wrote
who	wonder	wrung
whole	wondered	yards
whom	wonderful	year
whose	wondering	yes
why	won't	yet
wicker-covered	wood	yonder
wide	wooden	you
widened	woods	you'll
widow	woodwork	young
wife	word	younger
wild	words	your
wilder	wore	you're
wildest	work	yours
will	world	yourself
will be	worry	you've